A graduate of Hollins University, **Mary Burton** enjoys a variety of hobbies, including scuba diving, yoga and hiking. She is based in Richmond, Virginia, where she lives with her husband and two children.

MARY BURTON

THE
ARSONIST

MIRA

Published in Great Britain 2012
MIRA Books, an imprint of Harlequin (UK) Limited,
Eton House, 18-24 Paradise Road,
Richmond, Surrey, TW9 1SR

© Mary T. Burton 2006

ISBN 978 1 848 45103 2

58-0612

MIRA's policy is to use papers that are natural, renewable and recyclable products and made from wood grown in sustainable forests. The logging and manufacturing processes conform to the legal environmental regulations of the country of origin.

Printed and bound by
CPI Group (UK) Ltd, Croydon, CR0 4YY

Special thanks to
David S. "Steve" Parrott, Battalion Chief,
Emergency Operations, Chesterfield Fire
and Emergency Medical Services.

Prologue

Arson investigator Michael Gannon understood the obsession that drove arsonists to set fires. It was what made him good at what he did.

For seven months, he'd been tracking Nero, a monster who had set nine fires in the Washington, D.C. area, killed twelve people and destroyed millions of dollars in property. The metro area had been paralyzed with fear.

Now as Gannon stared down at the charred corpse the police believed was Nero, he couldn't quite believe the chase was over. He'd not anticipated this outcome. Nero had been his smartest opponent yet, and he'd never made a mistake—until last night.

The body lay curled in a fetal position near the back exit of the burned-out warehouse. The heat from the newly extinguished fire still radiated from the blackened concrete floor. The low, exuberant voices of police and fire crews buzzed around his head like flies. Reporters and curiosity seekers gathered fifty yards away on the other side of the yellow police tape.

As he studied the body's rigid arms covering an unrecognizable face, relief, anger, and yes, disappointment collided inside Gannon. He'd never get the chance to look the bastard in the eye or see him stand trial and face those he'd hurt.

"There's not much left of him," he said mainly to himself. If not for the evidence found in the back alley, he'd not have believed it was Nero.

The medical examiner, a thin woman with short black hair, dressed in a neat navy-blue pants suit, stood as she pulled off her rubber gloves. "Fifth- and sixth-degree burns nearly disintegrated him."

Gannon's sharp gaze rose to her angular face. "Can you ID him?"

She smiled at him and offered her hand. A flicker of attraction sparked in her eyes. "I'll ID him. Just give me a little time, Gannon."

He shook her hand, noted it was cold and then released it. He couldn't remember the woman's name and didn't have the energy to pretend he did. "Any thoughts to height, weight, race or age?"

She sighed, sensing he didn't notice her as a woman. "Definitely male. Maybe six feet. The rest will come when I do the autopsy."

"Thanks."

Folding his arms over his chest, Gannon watched the medical examiner make her final inspection of the corpse before ordering it moved to the body bag lying open on the floor.

Though it was only ten o'clock in the morning, Gannon's eyes itched with fatigue. He'd slept very little since the restaurant fire.

Fire Chief Jackson McCray, a tall redhead, lifted the crime scene tape and moved beside Gannon. "You look like hell."

Gannon tore his gaze from the body. "Right."

"What are you still doing here?" The chief's

slightly round belly strained against the buttons on his white uniform.

"I'm just seeing this through."

McCray watched as officers lowered the body into the body bag and zipped it closed.

Gannon reached in his pocket for his pack of cigarettes. "Not double-checking his escape route was stupid. That kind of mistake wasn't like Nero." He hated Nero but he had to respect his intellect and cunning. At first they'd thought the fire had been set by another arsonist because the location was so remote. Nero liked his fires closer to people, where they could generate the most hysteria.

However, the evidence was already piling up. "Did the accelerant found near the body match Nero's?"

"Sure did. This is our boy."

"I just can't believe he's dead."

"Believe it." McCray nodded toward the yellow tape that blocked off the crime scene. Beyond were dozens of television news crews and curiosity seekers. "Go home. Take a few weeks off."

Gannon felt at loose ends, oddly lost. "I don't

know what to do with myself without Nero to chase."

"Take that pretty wife of yours out to a fancy dinner."

Gannon pulled a cigarette out of the pack and then remembered he'd promised himself to give up smoking once Nero had been stopped. He shoved the pack back into his pocket. He'd made a lot of promises to himself these last few grueling months. Not only was he cutting the booze out, but he wasn't working any more twenty-hour days. He wanted his life back. "Amy left me two months ago." He spoke about the end of his five-year marriage as if it were the most mundane event. "The divorce will be final in a few months."

McCray's smile vanished. "I'm sorry. Why didn't you say something?"

"Nothing to say." He and Amy had fought a lot about his job. She'd wanted him to quit the department and sell plumbing supplies for his father.

Gannon watched the officers load the body bag onto the stretcher. They wheeled it over the warehouse floor toward the yellow police tape and the row of officers that kept the press away from the hearse.

TV cameras started rolling. A blond GQ-type stood in front of the Channel Five camera. He checked his hair seconds before his cameraman panned from the hearse to him. "Live from Shield's warehouse. The bloodthirsty arsonist is allegedly dead thanks to the brave efforts of our fire department's Michael Gannon who cornered the suspect last night in a final standoff."

Gannon had grown to despise Glass over the last six months. The reporter had gotten ahold of a sensitive detail of the investigation—Nero always included a pack of Rome matches with his letters. He'd reported it on the six o'clock news. After that, every nut in the city had started sending Gannon Rome matches.

Glass lapped up the extra attention. Ratings were all that mattered to him.

The reporter looked into the camera. "Gannon has worked round the clock for over six months, giving up his nights, weekends and even his marriage."

Disgust twisted in Gannon's gut. "He's painting me to be a hero."

"Like it or not you *are* a hero," McCray said.

"I'm no hero."

McCray knew Gannon well enough not to argue when he was in a foul mood. "Do you want me to make the statement to the media?"

"No. I'll wrap this one up." He glanced at the reporters, grateful this would be the last time he'd have to deal with them. "Chief, I'm also going to announce my retirement."

McCray froze. "What?"

"I quit. I'm done with this job. I've lost my edge."

"What do you mean? You cracked the Nero case."

"I didn't. Nero tripped up. I wonder now if I ever had what it took to catch him."

McCray rubbed the back of his neck. "You're being too hard on yourself. Hell, we all knew you were closing in on him. You just need some rest."

Gannon rubbed the thick stubble on his chin. "My mind is made up."

"Where are you going to go?"

It had been years since he'd slept the night

through or had drawn in a deep breath without the scents of fire. "I don't have a clue."

Where he went didn't matter now as long as he got away from this job, which was killing him by inches.

Nero wasn't dead.

He sat across town at the breakfast counter of a local diner sipping his coffee and watching the late-breaking news. The reporter was Stephen Glass, one of his favorites, and he was talking about Nero's unexpected death.

A dark-haired waitress, dressed in a white-and-blue uniform, refilled his cup. Following his line of sight to the television, she said, "So what's so important they got to break in on my game show?"

He glanced down at his coffee, slightly annoyed that the ratio of cream and coffee was now off. "The cops trapped Nero. He died in his latest fire."

She popped her gum. "No kidding."

He glanced at the waitress, annoyed by her loud gum chewing. He was looking forward to getting out of this city. It wasn't fun anymore. "Gannon closed the case."

"I knew he would." She waved over another waitress. "Betty, come look at the tube. The fire babe is on the air." The waitress winked at him. "Gannon is built like a brick house."

Betty joined her friend and the two women giggled like schoolgirls as Gannon gave his account of last night's fire.

Nero poured more cream into his coffee and carefully stirred it. Gannon was also smart. He'd been a worthy opponent, one who had kept him in the game far longer than was prudent.

Five nights ago, Gannon had missed him by seconds in the Adam's–Morgan restaurant fire. He'd known then that it was a matter of time before Gannon caught him.

The time had come to quit the game. As much as Nero loved the thrill of the chase and the exquisite way his fires danced, spending the rest of his life behind bars didn't appeal to him.

So, he'd found a homeless man in Lafayette Square, and lured him to the warehouse with the promise of money. He had given the man one hundred bucks and a bottle of MD 20/20. Nero had watched as the bum unscrewed the top and drank liberally from the bottle laced with drugs. Within minutes the bum had passed out.

Nero had dragged the man to the back entrance, doused him with accelerant, set the warehouse on fire and slipped into the shadows.

The cops had dutifully found all the clues he'd left behind including the duffel in the alley that was filled with Nero newspaper clippings.

The plan was perfect.

He was free.

For the first time in months, Nero felt relaxed and more at ease.

The itch to burn and destroy had vanished.

Nero sipped his coffee. It tasted good—the right balance of cream and coffee.

Maybe this time, he could quit setting fires and live a normal life.

Chapter 1

One Year Later

The informant's tip was explosive.

Excitement sizzled through Darcy Sampson's body as she stepped off the elevator into the *Washington Post*'s newsroom. She hurried to her desk. The large open room was full of desks, lined up one behind the other. Only inches separated hers from her colleague's.

Her computer screen was off. The desk was piled high with papers, reference books and, in the corner, a wilting plant.

Darcy dug her notebook out of her purse and

then dumped the bag in the bottom desk drawer. She couldn't wait to talk to her editor and pitch the story that would propel her byline from page twenty to the front page.

"So where's the fire?" The familiar raspy voice had Darcy looking up. Barbara Rogers, a fellow reporter, was wafer thin. Her salt-and-pepper hair was cut short and her wire-rimmed glasses magnified sharp gray eyes.

Darcy flipped her notebook open. She wanted to be sure of her facts before she talked to her editor. "Just kicking around a story idea."

Barbara had been in the business for thirty years. She knew all the angles. And she knew everything that went on in the newsroom. "Must be some story. You look like you're about to start salivating."

Darcy didn't dare confirm or deny. "I've got to run."

Barbara wasn't offended. "Sure, cut your best friend out of the loop."

Best friend. Barbara had stolen two story ideas from her in the last year. She hurried toward her editor's office. Visions of a Pulitzer prize and national exposure danced in her head. Through the glass walls of his office, she could see Paul Tyler was on the phone, but she knocked anyway.

What she had was too good to wait.

The phone cradled under his ear, Paul glanced up at her. He looked annoyed but motioned her inside.

Darcy hurried into the cramped office littered with stacks of newspapers, magazines and piles of books on the floor. She moved the books from the chair in front of his desk and sat down. The heavy scent of cigarettes hung in the air. He wasn't supposed to smoke in the building, but that didn't stop him from putting duct tape over the smoke detector and sneaking a cigarette once in a while.

Paul pinched the bridge of his nose. A swath of graying hair hung over his tired green eyes. "Right, well, do the best you can. And call me if you find another lead." Hanging up the receiver, he sighed as he looked up at Darcy. "What is it, Sampson?"

She sucked in a deep, calming breath, willing herself to talk slowly. "I have a story."

He stared at her blankly. "And?"

Darcy leaned forward. "Remember Nero?"

Paul sat back in his chair. A dollop of ketchup stained the right pocket of his shirt. "Sure. The arsonist that tried to torch D.C. last year. Killed twelve people."

"Right."

Paul glanced at the pile of papers on his desk as if the conversation was already losing him. "He died in one of his own fires."

She spoke softly. "What if he didn't die?"

He looked up. Interest mingled with doubt in his eyes. "He died. The fire department and police department had mountains of information on the guy…Raymond somebody."

"Mason. Raymond Mason." She flipped her notebook open and searched several pages before she found the right reference. "He was a homeless man. Also, a college graduate and Gulf War vet. Volunteer firefighter."

"Right. I remember now. So why should I care about all this?"

"I got a call from a woman yesterday. She is Raymond's sister, Sara Highland."

"Why would she call you?"

A valid question. Until now, all Darcy had covered were city planning and council meetings. "My ex-boyfriend, Stephen." She hated giving Stephen-the-creep any credit for the tip, but he had been the reason Sara had contacted her. Stephen, a reporter for TV Five News, had made quite a name for himself covering the Nero fires. "He interviewed Sara last year and thinking she might remember something of interest, he had given her his home number—which in fact was my number because he was basically living at my place most of the time. Anyway, she called. When I played back Sara's message on my answering machine, I knew I had to talk to her."

Paul's glazed look was a signal that she was rambling. "Get to the punch line."

"Sara doesn't believe that Raymond was Nero. She believes he was set up."

Paul yawned. "She said this last year. And who could blame her? No one wants to believe their brother is a serial arsonist and murderer."

"This time she's got facts to back up her statements." Darcy flipped through a couple of pages in her notebook. "It took Sara time get over the shock of it all. When she did, she started talking to the men who knew Raymond."

He lifted a brow. "Homeless men?"

"Yes. There was one man in particular—a Bud Jones. He was a veteran, too. He and Raymond were good friends. I went to talk to him. Bud said a week before the last fire a well-dressed man stopped and talked to Raymond. The two hit it off and the stranger gave Raymond five dollars. The guy came back several more times over the next few days. Finally, he offered big money to Raymond for a job."

"What kind of job?"

"Raymond never said." She scooted to the edge of her seat. "But Bud thinks it had to do with Nero's last fire."

"Did Sara or you pay this Bud character money for information?" There was no missing his cynicism. Paul believed Bud had simply told Sara what she wanted to hear in exchange for money.

"I tried to give him a twenty but he wouldn't take it."

"Where's Bud been all this time? Why hasn't anyone else mentioned him?"

"He took off the day before the last fire. Thumbed down to Florida where he stayed until last month."

Paul steepled his fingers. "Keep talking."

"Raymond was supposed to meet the stranger at Shield's warehouse."

That had Paul's attention. "The spot of Nero's last fire."

"Where Raymond died." She closed her notebook. "I think Raymond was set up by the real Nero. I think the real Nero knew the police and arson investigators were on to him and that if he didn't do something quickly, he'd be caught."

"Great theory, but where's the proof?"

"I don't have it, yet, but I intend to get it."

"Where?"

"Remember Michael Gannon?"

"Sure, chief arson investigator on the case. Dropped off the scene after Nero's death was confirmed."

"I talked to a couple of buddies of his in the department. I said I was doing a year anniversary thing on the fires. Anyway, one let it slip that Gannon never really believed Nero was dead.

When I questioned him further, he started back-pedaling."

"Where's Gannon now?"

"He moved down to Preston Springs, Virginia, and opened a motorcycle shop."

"Aren't you from Preston Springs?"

Darcy's stomach tightened. That was the major fly in the ointment. She and her mother didn't get on so well. And the last time she'd been home had been a year ago for her father's funeral. "Yeah."

"So what are you going to do—interview Gannon?"

"If it were only that easy. Gannon hates report-ers. Which we can thank Stephen for."

Paul rubbed the back of his neck with his hand. "Stephen did harass the hell out of Gannon."

"Made his life rough. I'm afraid if Gannon knows I had anything to do with Stephen, reporting or Nero he'd shut me down."

He drummed his fingers on his desk. "So what do you want from me?"

"Like you said, I'm from Preston Springs. I can go home under the guise of visiting my mother and brother. And while I'm there, make contact with Gannon. With any luck, he'll open up."

Paul folded his fingers over his chest. "Long shot, if you ask me."

She rubbed her palms together. "But you've got to admit, it's worth the chance. If we could prove Nero didn't die, the coverage would be incredible. We'd get picked up all over the country. All I need is two weeks."

He nodded. "It damn sure would be." He sighed staring at the stacks of paper on his desk. "I can't give you two weeks. Only a week."

Darcy swallowed a smile. She had Paul. Now it was a matter of reeling him in. "Ten days."

"Eight."

"Nine."

He glared at her. "Sold. But this adventure is on your dime until you come up with something hard."

She jumped to her feet. "No problem. I'll leave first thing in the morning."

Standing, he held up his hand to stop her. "I want you to keep me posted. Call me every day or two. Gannon won't be easy to crack. Can be a real son of a bitch from what I remember."

"I'm not afraid of him."

"You should be."

Just the idea of this story had her nerves humming. "Michael Gannon will talk to me. I can guarantee it."

Chapter 2

The perky *Surprise, I'm home!* Darcy Sampson had practiced on the car ride down Interstate 81 died on her lips when she saw flames shooting out of a frying pan on her family's restaurant's industrial kitchen stove.

For a moment, she stood, dumbstruck, her green duffel bag gripped in her hand as flames licked the sides of the stove's greasy exhaust hood and black smoke filled the restaurant kitchen.

"Fire!" Darcy shouted.

Her mother, a short plump woman with graying hair, whirled around from the sink where she'd been washing dishes. Panicking, she grabbed a full glass of water and raced toward the fire.

Darcy dropped her bags. "No, Mom, don't!"

Her mother tossed the cold water on the hot grease in the pan. Immediately, the fire exploded higher, spilling over the sides of the stove. Hot oil spattered like a Roman candle. Mrs. Sampson screamed and jumped back as oil peppered her arm.

The smoke detector started to screech through the entire building. Darcy ran down the shotgun style kitchen to the pantry. There she grabbed a large box of flour and rushed toward the blaze. Without hesitating, she dumped the entire box on the flames. The fire died instantly.

Her heart pounding, Darcy set the empty tub down on the island in the center of the kitchen and rubbed a shaking hand to her forehead. "Mom, you know how to put out a grease fire." White flour coated Darcy's fingers, the stove and the mud-brown linoleum floor. She looked down at her black silk pants suit now dusted with flour. "I just had this dry-cleaned."

Her mother glanced impatiently up at the smoke detector that still wailed. She started to wave her apron in the air under the blaring smoke detector. "Help me turn this thing off. I don't need the fire department knocking on my door."

Darcy grabbed a stepladder, and in high heeled boots climbed up the steps and disconnected the smoke detector. She pulled the battery out of the back of it. Blessed silence filled the room.

Darcy climbed down and shut off the gas to the burner under the frying pan now covered with a thick coat of flour. She set down the battery and faced her mother. "Did you burn yourself?"

Her mother pursed her lips. "I'm fine."

The speckled burns on her mother's arms said otherwise. Darcy went to the sink, turned on the tap and soaked a handful of paper towels in the cool water. She rang out the excess water.

"Let me see your arms."

"I'm fine," her mother said, her tone brusque.

Darcy swallowed her frustration and took her mother's arm in hand. Gently she started to clean her arm.

Her mother winced. "That hurts. Don't be so rough."

"You need some antibiotic ointment on that."

Her mother pulled her arm away. "It's not that bad."

She'd been home less than two minutes and already she and her mother were arguing. It had to be a record. "Mom, you wouldn't admit to third-degree burns even if they covered your body."

Mrs. Sampson took the towels from Darcy. "I've managed to take care of myself all these years while you've been up north with your big city job."

Darcy's defenses rose. But instead of taking the bait, she went to the swinging doors that led to the dining room so that she could calm the customers.

To her surprise, the row of booths covered in green vinyl and the seats around the mahogany bar were empty.

She checked her watch. Two o'clock. The lunch hour had passed, but normally there'd be a half a dozen folks eating a late lunch.

As she glanced around the deserted room, she realized the place hadn't changed in twenty years. It still smelled of stale cigarettes and beer and was decorated with her brother's football memorabilia, including jerseys from his peewee days through his brief time with the Pittsburgh Steelers.

Growing up, Darcy had jokingly called the room *The Shrine,* though deep inside it hurt knowing her parents' world revolved solely around her brother. She'd been all but invisible to them.

"Where is everyone?" she asked. She ignored the tightness in her chest and walked back into the kitchen.

"We don't open for lunch anymore." Her mother surveyed the mess around the stove as she pushed a trembling hand through her short gray hair. "We open at five now."

That surprised her. "Why? The lunch crowd was always profitable."

Her mother got a broom from a small closet by the back door. "Trevor says lunch is more trouble than it is worth. The real money is made at dinner and the bar."

Her brother, Trevor, had become the tavern manager after their father's death last year. Trevor had just been cut from the Steelers and was at loose ends. At the time, his managing the restaurant had seemed like a win-win solution for everyone.

"Dad never missed an opportunity to make

money. He only closed on Christmas Day. Trevor's decision must have Dad rolling in his grave."

Jan Sampson shot an annoyed glance her daughter's way. She wasn't willing to discuss Trevor's managerial decisions. But instead of saying so, she diverted the conversation to another topic. "Good Lord, I've never seen a fire jump like that."

Darcy could feel a headache coming on. "I get the hint—Trevor is perfect." It had been six years since she'd moved away from home, but it surprised her how deep old resentments still ran.

Her mother ignored the comment.

Darcy drew in a calming breath. This visit home was going to work. "What caused the fire, Mom?"

Her mother tugged down the edges of her Steelers yellow T-shirt. "I was frying potatoes when I noticed there were dishes to be put away. I got distracted. The next thing I know, you're screaming fire."

"You could have burned the whole place down."

Anger flashed in her mother's eyes. "What are you doing here anyway?"

Darcy pushed aside her annoyance. She'd come home for a story—not a tender family reunion. "I was fired." The lie tumbled over her lips easily. She'd decided on the drive down that honesty wasn't the best policy if she were going to get Gannon to talk to her. Her mother couldn't keep a secret.

Mrs. Sampson stopped her sweeping. "Fired?"

Darcy shoved her hands in her pockets. She'd rehearsed this conversation on the drive down. "A week ago."

"You were always in the center of trouble as a kid."

"Straight As was how I remember it," she said, her anger rising. "And I worked in our family's restaurant full time all the way through college."

Mrs. Sampson ignored what Darcy had said. "Why did they fire you?"

There was no point arguing. "I wrote an exposé on a developer. He used shoddy materials in his buildings. Turns out he was a major advertiser with the paper. I refused to drop the story. I got fired." It all had sounded plausible when she'd made it up, but now she found she had trouble meeting her mother's gaze.

Mrs. Sampson started to sweep up the burned

flour, again. "That doesn't make sense. I see your name in the paper a lot. Your articles are good enough."

Unreasonably pleased, she stood a little taller. "You get *The Post*?"

Mrs. Sampson shrugged. "From time to time. I buy it from the drugstore."

Darcy stood five inches taller than her mother, yet she still felt like a five-year-old at times. "Any articles you liked in particular?"

"No. Would you get the dustpan?"

Grateful for the task, she dug the pan out of the broom closet and knelt down so her mother could sweep the pile of flour onto the pan.

"You should have listened to your boss, Darcy."

Darcy picked up the full pan and dumped it in the trash can. "You're right."

Her mother studied her an extra beat as if she wasn't sure if Darcy was being sarcastic or not. Darcy tried to look sincere.

Mrs. Sampson softened a fraction. "What about that boyfriend of yours?"

"We broke up almost a year ago."

Mrs. Sampson swept up the rest of the flour and

dumped it into the trash can. "I saw that Stephen guy on the *Today Show* when he was reporting on those fires in Washington last year. I thought his smile was too quick."

"And fake too. Would you believe he spent thousands on caps?" His new, rich girlfriend had paid for them. "I still can't believe I wasted two years with him."

Mrs. Sampson shook her head. "So you've nowhere else to go and you've come home."

Pride had her lifting her chin a notch. "I know I've not been the best daughter. Dad and I fought so much and I didn't even stay for the reception after the funeral."

The apology caught Mrs. Sampson by surprise. More tension drained from her shoulders. "Your father wasn't the easiest man either, Darcy. I knew he could be difficult."

An unexpected lump formed in her throat. "I was hoping I could crash here for a while."

Mrs. Sampson was silent for a moment. "Of course, you can stay here for a while. In fact, I've an opening for a waitress. Our waitress quit just yesterday. I'll have to check with Trevor of course, but I don't see why you couldn't work the tables like you used to."

"That would be great." The idea of working in the restaurant didn't appeal, but it would be the perfect cover story.

Her mother nodded. "You can start by taking out this trash. Then, when you get your bags put away, you can start prepping for the dinner crowd. My cook, George, is on break now but he'll be back within the hour."

"George? What happened to Dave?" Dave had cooked for the Varsity since she'd been in elementary school.

Mrs. Sampson sighed. "He quit about six months ago."

There was a time when she'd known everything about the Varsity. Now she was the outsider. "Everything all right with him?"

She stood a little straighter. "He just wanted more money than we could pay."

"That doesn't sound like Dave." The tall, lean man always enjoyed a good joke and kept Eskimo Pies for Darcy in the freezer.

"People change."

The tone in her mother's voice told her not to push. "Okay. Where is Trevor? I tried him on his cell phone earlier but he didn't pick up."

"Your brother is getting supplies for the dinner crowd. We ran short on a few things."

"How's he doing?"

Mrs. Sampson started to wipe the cooktop with a rag. "He's doing just fine. The tavern has never been busier. Thank God, I have him."

Darcy didn't miss the hidden meaning. Trevor was the golden child. "Good."

"Well, you better get to work," her mother said. "That trash won't take itself out."

Darcy glanced at the trash can overflowing with debris. She visualized the story she was going to write and the awards she was going to win.

"Will do." Darcy sealed up the green bag lining the wheeled plastic trash can.

"And when you're done with that, get this kitchen cleaned."

"Right."

Darcy pushed up the sleeves of her suit and tried to pull the bag out. It was heavier than she realized. Deciding to keep the trash bag in the can, she tipped the can back on its wheels and started to pull it outside.

"Darcy?" Her mother looked as if she had something else to say.

"Yeah?"

As their gazes met, her mother frowned, seeming to change her mind. "Never mind."

"Okay." Drawing in a deep breath, Darcy yanked at the can again and slowly started to drag it to the back alley behind the Varsity.

The alley was lined with pitted asphalt and wide enough for cars to drive through. The Varsity, flanked by a bridal shop and a drugstore, was located in middle of the block. The battered blue Dumpster, shared by all three businesses, was tucked in a nook by the drugstore.

Darcy pulled the trash can down the two steps by the back door, wincing as it banged hard with each drop. Her ankles wobbled as her high heeled boots caught between two of the cobblestones. Cursing, she yanked it free, and in the process, ripped the leather from one heel.

She stared at the torn Italian leather. The three-hundred-dollar boots had been a Christmas gift from Stephen two years ago. She suspected this was fate's retribution for the lies she'd told her mother.

Tracking down the real Nero was worth it, she reminded herself.

Standing taller, she gripped the handle of the trash can and started down the alley. "I'm not going to quit. I'm not. I will get through this."

The heavy can rumbled over the uneven asphalt as she headed toward the Dumpster. She opened the side door of the Dumpster and tugged on the green trash bag three times but couldn't get it free.

"You are a stupid trash bag," she said gritting her teeth. "And you aren't going to win." Determined, she jerked the bag. Her fitted jacket strained against her back and she pulled and pulled until finally the garbage bag wiggled free. She dumped the bag into the Dumpster.

Taking out the trash was hardly a moment to be celebrated, but she did feel a little pang of pride as she brushed her hands together. *Tenacity.* It had won out over the trash and it would find Nero.

Her shoulders back, she started to drag the can back to the kitchen. She was so lost in her own thoughts that she didn't hear the roar of the motorcycle zooming down the alley until it was almost too late.

The driver hit the brakes and narrowly swerved around her as she looked up. Shocked, she stumbled back.

Her heart hammering in her chest, she went from fear to anger in a split second. Without thinking, she flipped the Motorcycle Man the bird. "What is the matter with you, sport?"

Motorcycle Man shoved up his visor. Electric blue eyes that held no hint of emotion stared at her.

Suddenly, all her senses became very sharp. She was intensely aware of the hot June air and the sweat drizzling down her chest between her breasts.

The jolt of desire surprised and irritated her. The guy had almost run her over. If she'd had any sense, she'd not have taken on a redneck biker in an alley. But her nerves were shot and her mouth worked faster than her brain. "Hey, mister, do you think you can be a little more careful?"

"You're the one that wasn't watching where you were going." His voice was hoarse, rusty and sent tremors down her spine.

Still, Darcy marched toward him, pulling her

trash can with her. The idea of coming home had frayed her nerves and she realized she was spoiling for a fight. "This is an alleyway! It's not meant for high-speed chases. You could have flattened me like a pancake."

"You smell like smoke."

"What?"

He looked around the alleyway. "What was burning?"

She nodded her head toward the restaurant kitchen's door. "A grease fire in the Varsity's kitchen. It's out now."

His gaze sharpened. "They had another one?"

Another one? What was happening to that place? When she'd been kid growing up and working there, they'd never had any trouble. Family loyalty had her keeping those thoughts to herself. "Like I said, it's under control."

His gloved leather hand tightened around the bike's throttle. "So are you going to be okay, or do I have to call an ambulance?"

His sarcasm grated her nerves. "I'll probably have nightmares for a month."

Creases formed around his eyes, a sign he was

grinning. "So are you the new waitress at the Varsity?"

"How do you know that?"

"Who else would be hauling around a trash can with the *Varsity* stenciled on it?"

She glanced at the faded lettering. "Right."

"You don't look like a waitress."

"I'll take that as a compliment." She sounded bitchy—even to her own ears.

"Right. Well, sorry for the scare." He flipped his visor down. "Watch where you are walking. You might not be so lucky next time."

She gritted her teeth. "Drive more slowly!"

Laughter rumbled deep in his chest. "Try not to frighten the customers away."

The laughter in his voice irritated her. "I'm a *good* waitress."

"Right." He revved the engine loudly and then slowly drove down the alley.

Muttering an oath under her breath, Darcy started back toward the Varsity.

She'd gone two feet when her high heel caught between cobblestones again and she stumbled. Gripping the handle of the trash can, she glanced back to make sure Motorcycle Man had left. He had.

With as much dignity as she could muster, she brushed her bangs off her face, and dragging the trash can behind her, retreated back into the kitchen.

Darcy shut the kitchen door and leaned against it. Closing her eyes, she let a sigh shudder through her body as she thought about Motorcycle Man's laughing gaze. It seemed everyone had questioned her competency since she had arrived in Preston Springs.

But she'd prove them all wrong—when she found Nero.

Chapter 3

Darcy spent the next half hour unpacking and changing into a cotton T-shirt, jeans and running shoes. She itched to go out for a long run before reviewing her notes on Nero, but it was already past three in the afternoon and the dinner crowd would be arriving at five o'clock.

As she brushed her hair up into a ponytail, she glanced around her old bedroom. Her mother had taken down her posters and painted over the purple. Her brass daybed was still there, but the black-and-white comforter was gone and in its place a green quilt and lots of pillows. Her mother's sewing machine sat in the corner next to a white glider and footstool.

Her mother had done a good job of erasing any signs that her daughter had ever lived in this house. None of this would have bothered Darcy, if not for Trevor's shrine in the diner.

"And why do you care?" Darcy mumbled as she tightened the rubber band around the thick handful of hair. "This is just a temporary stop. Deal with it."

She started down the back staircase that led to the kitchen. As she approached the last step, she heard a man singing "When the Saints Come Marching In." The voice was deep, the tone so off-key it made her smile.

Darcy found a stocky man standing in front of the stove stirring a pot of chili. He wore a white cook's uniform with the sleeves rolled up over tattooed forearms. A rawhide strip held back thinning gray hair in a tight ponytail.

"Hey," she said. Her mother had told her the tavern had a new cook. His name was George Paris.

George didn't look up. "What did you do to my

kitchen?" Each word was coated in a thick Alabama accent.

Darcy glanced around and seeing no signs of her mother assumed the comment was directed at her. "Saved it."

"It took me a half hour just to clean the flour out of the burner."

The chili smelled good and she remembered she'd not eaten since breakfast. "You're lucky to have a burner or a job for that matter. If I hadn't shown up, Mom would have torched the place."

Nodding thoughtfully, he tossed a handful of chili powder into the pot. If he'd worked here six months, he knew her mother could be a bit scattered at times. "Then I owe you my thanks. Unemployment doesn't suit me so well."

She snagged an apple from a bowl of fruit on the island. "Me either."

He studied her, his eyes narrowing slightly. "Your mother said you are the new waitress."

"That's right." She bit into the apple.

"You don't look like your mother or Trevor."

The apple tasted tart. "I take after my father."

Eyeing her one last second, he turned back to his

chili. "You can start making the dinner salads. Lettuce, two tomatoes, cucumber and three red onion rings."

"I know the drill. I've made a million of those in my past life here." Holding the apple in her teeth she washed and dried her hands. She took another bite of apple set it aside and crossed to the refrigerator. She pulled out a bag of precut lettuce, a box of cherry tomatoes, a cucumber and red onions. She set it all down on the island.

"Remember, only three slices of cucumber per plate," he said.

She set the apple aside. "Tomatoes on the left, cucumbers in the middle, onions on the right. I remember." She grabbed a stack of plates from the shelf on the wall above the sink and started to line them up assembly line fashion. She hated having to deal with this mundane stuff while knowing Nero could be alive, but for now she had to make like a waitress so no one would suspect her motives.

"Where is Trevor? Shouldn't he be here now?" she asked.

He crushed a handful of dried red pepper flakes in his hand then dumped them into the pot. "He called your mother and said that he'll be back by five o'clock."

She noted a hint of irritation in his voice. "Trevor likes to play it fast and loose. Deadlines don't get to him. Used to irritate his football coaches no end."

"Then he is in the wrong business." George sounded annoyed. "Restaurants are nothing but deadlines."

"Mom says the business is doing well." She kept her voice neutral, but she was fishing. Natural curiosity had been one of the reasons she'd become a reporter.

George shrugged. "I don't think about things like that as long as I get paid on time."

"Which you do?" She figured she had a right to know how Trevor ran the place.

"Most times."

Frowning, she tore into the lettuce. She'd hoped when Trevor had taken over the restaurant that he'd grow up and become more responsible.

Let it go, Darcy. This gig was strictly a stepping-stone to her Pulitzer. "And Mom is where?"

"She is rolling the napkins and checking the bar."

"Okay." Darcy set out thirty plates on the center

island. As she started to lay torn lettuce leaves on each, a truck pulled up in the back alley.

George wiped his hands on his apron and glanced out the screened door. "It's about time Thompsons got here. We are just about out of everything." He went to the door and waved. "Hey, Harvey. You can bring our order right in. We've got to get those chickens started if they're going to be ready on time."

Harvey Thompson, a tall thin man in his mid-fifties, came in the back door, with only a clipboard in his hand. He glanced over at Darcy. "Hey, Darcy, when did you get back in town?"

She grinned. "Just today."

"You look good. You lose weight?"

She smiled. "Sure did. Twenty pounds this last year. Thanks for noticing."

George looked impatient. "Harvey, you can start unloading any time."

But the man hesitated. "I'm going to need a check from Trevor."

"What do you mean—we have to pay C.O.D., Harvey? You always bill us," George said.

Harvey's face turned red. "You're behind."

George muttered a curse. "I'm a cook, not a bookkeeper. I shouldn't have to deal with these kinds of things when I got a roomful of customers showing up in less than two hours. Wait right here." He stormed into the dining room in search of Darcy's mother.

Harvey glanced awkwardly at Darcy. "I knew this wasn't going to be easy. But my boss said no cash, no delivery."

"Trevor that far behind?" Darcy said.

Before Harvey could answer, George returned with Mrs. Sampson. "Tell Mrs. S. what you just told me."

Harvey's face reddened as he addressed Mrs. Sampson. "I'm going to need cash on delivery today, Jan. No money, no food."

Her mother's laugh had an edge. "That can't be right, Harvey. I know Trevor just sent you in a check last week."

"It bounced," Harvey said in a low voice.

"It didn't bounce," Mrs. Sampson said. "I made a huge deposit only last week into the account."

Harvey shrugged. "I don't know what to say. All I know is no cash, no delivery."

Her mother looked flustered and embarrassed now. "This has to be a mistake."

Darcy stepped forward. "How much would you need today to make your delivery?"

"If it were anybody else, I'd need it all. But seeing as it's y'all, I'll take a thousand. I figure this is just a paperwork glitch."

Her mother had never been one to handle the business end of the diner. Her father had while he was alive, and since his death, Trevor had.

"I don't keep that kind of money in my personal account," Mrs. Sampson said.

"I can bring the order back tomorrow," Harvey said.

"We need today's order or we won't be able to open tonight," George said.

"Don't know what to say," Harvey said. He looked as if he'd just endured root canal work.

The last thing Darcy wanted was to be drawn further into tavern business. She only had twelve hundred in her checking account and most of that was earmarked for her credit card bill, which was due at the end of next week. Since she'd dropped the twenty pounds this year, she'd splurged on new clothes—a lot of new clothes.

But high interest rates and minimum payments aside, if the Varsity went down, so would her cover. "I can go to the bank and pull the cash out of my account. I'm going to need to be paid back by Monday, Mom."

Mrs. Sampson looked relieved. "Trevor will pay you back as soon as he gets here."

Darcy nodded. "Harvey, go ahead and start unloading. I'll be back with the cash in five minutes."

He hesitated. "Okay."

Despite her mother's assurance, she felt as if she'd just stepped in quicksand. She got her purse and headed out the back alley, this time looking both ways.

Once Harvey was paid, Darcy, George and her mother focused on prepping for the dinner crowd. The Varsity didn't have any other staff so the pace was quick and the work more physically challenging than she remembered. Still, despite a few dropped plates, she, George and her mother were ready by the time five o'clock rolled around. There was still no sign of Trevor.

Oddly enough, before her mother flipped the Closed sign to Open she felt as jittery as when she'd turned in her first article. So much was riding on her getting information from Gannon on Nero.

Thoughts of Nero vanished when the customers started arriving right at five. Within an hour, the diner was buzzing. All fifteen booths were filled and she and her mother ran from table to table taking orders, refilling drinks and serving entrées. To her surprise, she remembered more and more as the evening progressed. She'd forgotten how good she was at working this place.

She thought about Motorcycle Man. If he saw her in action now, he'd be eating his words.

By eight o'clock, most of the regulars were sitting at the bar. There was Chief Wheeler, the town's fire chief who was in his late forties. Chief's hair was thinning and he'd grown paunchy in the last six years. Next to him sat a friend of hers from high school, Larry White, a tall, lean truck driver who worked for a wholesale electronics distributor.

"So your mom says you got canned," Larry said to Darcy.

For the sake of the Nero investigation she wanted to downplay her reporting background. Folks had a way of clamming up when they knew a reporter, even a supposedly ex-reporter, was around. "Hey, do me a favor guys and drop the subject. Kinda touchy."

Larry and the chief nodded thoughtfully.

"Will do. Been fired myself a couple of times," Larry said. He sipped his cola. "It bites."

"We can keep a secret," the chief said.

"Thanks."

Minutes later, a tall, lean man walked into the tavern. In his forties, he was very athletic and had thick blonde hair. He wore thin wire-rimmed glasses. He took a seat beside Larry and held out a smooth hand to the trucker who took it immediately. "How's it going?"

"Can't complain, Nathan," Larry said. "Nathan, I'd like you to meet Darcy Sampson. Her family's owned the Varsity for years and she's back working at her old job."

Nathan smiled at Darcy. "Pleasure."

His gaze possessed an intensity that made her believe for an instant that she was the only person in the room. There was no denying he was a very attractive man. She sucked in her stomach. "Can I get you anything to drink?"

"Coffee."

"Sure thing," she said. She sounded cool, but for some reason he jumbled her nerves. *Cup. Coffeepot. Pour.* She poured him a cup and set it in front of him. "Cream? Sugar?"

The faint lines at his temples deepened when he smiled. "No thanks." He sipped his coffee. "Good. So, you just start?"

"Tonight's my first night." Darcy felt herself blushing. "So, Chief, how did your day go?"

The chief grimaced. "We had one hell of a fire."

Nathan's face was blank. "I've been at the construction site all day. What's the scoop?"

The chief leaned forward. "The Super 8 burned to the ground. Worst fire I've seen in years. Started in a storage closet and then quickly spread to the building's roof. We evacuated the motel and put our hoses on the fire. But the damn thing wouldn't go out. Within thirty minutes, the motel was burned to the ground."

Darcy's heart started to pound in her chest. The fire likely had nothing to do with Nero, but it was strange that the chief had battled an intense fire the day she arrived to investigate a serial arsonist.

Nathan sipped his coffee. "Do you know what started it?"

The chief shook his head. "Don't know. We got the arson boys from Roanoke coming in tomorrow."

Darcy lingered.

"You think someone set the fire on purpose?" Larry asked.

"No, I doubt it. Likely someone did something stupid," the chief said. "They'll have a report for us in a couple of days."

Larry pulled a toothpick from his pocket and popped it into his mouth. "Bet it was teen gangs."

Chief Wheeler laughed. "Larry you got teen gangs on the brain since you saw that *20/20* show last month."

George rang a bell, which told Darcy another order was up. Swallowing an oath, she picked up the order and took the plates to table number six. By the time she'd gotten them ketchup and refilled their colas, the men at the bar were talking about another fire.

Darcy topped up the chief's drink. "You get a lot of fires in the area?"

The chief shrugged. "Not many as a rule."

Darcy held up the pitcher of cola. "Like a refill, Larry?"

"Not yet," he said smiling.

"So how do you like Preston Springs so far, Nathan?" She wanted to stay in on this conversation without being too obvious.

Nathan sipped his coffee. "Love it."

She held up the coffeepot. "So you're working on the condo project off I-81?"

He held up his cup. "That's right."

She refilled it. Given time, she'd crack this Nero case. There was a story here and she could feel it in her bones. "Long hours?"

He nodded his thanks. "Always."

George rang his bell and Darcy had to abandon her conversation and serve another customer.

Given time. Who was she kidding? She barely had time to pee.

It was nine o'clock before Darcy could pull her head above water again to think. Nathan, the chief and Larry had left and there was still no sign of Trevor.

Her feet ached from running from table to table. If her brother had been here, she'd have had more time to talk to the chief, maybe find out something about Michael Gannon. But Trevor was nowhere in sight.

At nine forty-five, she'd not had a break and was starving. She'd eaten three large handfuls of the cocktail nuts—a good four hundred calories by her way of thinking. At the rate she was going, she'd weigh two hundred pounds before she got back to D.C. When the guy at table seven sent his order back for the third time, she vowed to skin Trevor alive when he did arrive.

At ten, the crowd had turned over several times. Folks looking for a meal had long cleared out. Most were now there for drinks.

At ten-fifteen, the front door opened and to her great relief, Trevor strolled in. Everyone at the bar and the booths waved him a greeting as he flashed his million-dollar smile. Trevor, tall and muscular with thick brown hair, kissed his mother, who beamed up at him from her current post at the cash register, and then strolled over to the bar as if he had all the time in the world.

When he spotted Darcy, his grin widened. "Mom said you were back."

"Man, it's about time you got here," she said as she stuck a lime in a Gin Fizz and handed it to a customer at the bar.

He studied her trim figure. "You've lost weight."

That compliment was her Achilles' heel and she immediately started to thaw. "Yeah."

Trevor opened his arms wide. "Is that the nicest thing you can say to your baby brother?"

Darcy really wanted to stay mad at Trevor. He'd left her in the lurch for most of the evening. But there was something about Trevor and his natural charm. She couldn't stay mad at him.

She stepped into his arms and hugged him. He wrapped his long arms around her and squeezed her tight against him. He smelled of cigarettes and beer, but in all honesty, she'd never felt more welcome than she did at this moment.

Since her breakup with Stephen, there'd been no one to hug or comfort her or tell her that everything was going to be all right after a bad day. Trevor's hug made up for all of that. For just a split second, she felt safe, secure and loved. And for that she could forgive him almost anything.

Darcy choked back the tears crowding her throat and pulled back. "It's good to see you."

His smile lit up his eyes. "You too. So who's the bastard that fired my big sister? I want a name because I'm going to have to rough him up."

Darcy laughed and tears did fill her eyes this time. "Thanks, but I got it under control."

"It wouldn't be any trouble at all, Dee. I can drive up to D.C., pound some flesh and be home before you know it."

Gratitude choked her throat. "Just the offer makes me feel better."

He hugged her again before he released her. "It's a standing offer." He moved behind the bar and drafted himself a beer. He took a long drink, nearly draining half the mug. "Hey, thanks for covering the delivery today. I don't know what happened with the payment. But I'll write you a check first thing in the morning."

"Thanks." Darcy smiled. "So when did you start drinking?" Their dad had been an alcoholic, and, like her, Trevor had always sworn to stay off the sauce.

He rolled his eyes. "A half a beer is hardly a drinking problem, Dee."

"That's what Dad used to say."

Michael Gannon often lost track of time when he was working on a new bike. Regularly, he worked hours under the garage's fluorescent glare often skipping meals. Tonight, however, he was having trouble concentrating. He kept thinking about the fire at the Super 8. The fire at the motel possessed an intensity that had surprised him. An older hotel could easily have burned that fast, but new construction rarely did.

He shut off the flame of his blowtorch and set it and the solder down on the workbench next to the gas tank he was fabricating. He pulled off his faceplate and stepped back, easing the kinks from his back as he moved. He'd been working on a custom gas tank for a vintage old-school bike most of the day. The task should have taken a few hours. But his concentration kept wavering and he'd been forced to work well into the night to finish it.

The bike was expected to go to the paint shop in six days, and if he didn't get it built in time, he'd fall behind schedule.

He picked up the tank and studied the cigar-shaped form. The seams and edges were rough now, but tomorrow he'd buff out the uneven spots. And once painted, it would be sweet.

Gannon set the tank down and walked over to the long window of his shop. Outside, the bulb above his front door cast a ring of light. Across the street, the neon lights of the Varsity tavern blinked. The tavern was winding down and the last customers made their way out the front door.

Thinking about their new waitress, he went outside. She had a real mouth on her, but he still couldn't help but grin when he pictured her green eyes blazing at him.

He glanced again at the Varsity and then checked his watch. The tavern was open for another fifteen minutes, enough time to get a bite to eat. But he didn't like being close to cigarettes when he was this edgy. He'd not had a cigarette in a year and he wasn't going to mess up just because some fool had set an accidental fire.

A bike ride was in order. He needed to get out in the open air and let the wind clear the cobwebs from his brain. As he started back inside to get his bike, the leggy waitress pushed through the front door of the tavern. She had her arm around a guy who was clearly drunk.

Gannon paused, stepping back into the shadows. He imagined the waitress had handled her share of drunks, but he hung around in case there was trouble.

The waitress and her customer stood outside the tavern and he suspected they were waiting for a cab. The drunk swayed a couple of times and then his right hand drifted up to the waitress's butt. She slapped it down.

Gannon grinned.

When the cab arrived, the brunette helped the drunk into the cab. She leaned in the backseat window, her ponytail swishing forward over her shoulder as she bade him good evening. When the cab drove off, she waved.

He watched her walk back toward the bar, admiring the way her jeans hugged her rear. He couldn't resist stepping partway into the light and shouting, "Break any plates tonight?"

She whirled around searching the darkness until she saw him. For a moment she stared as if she didn't know him and then she connected the dots. "Six. Run over any more people today?"

He laughed. "You're it so far."

Unexpectedly, she smiled. The smile lit up her face, making Gannon very aware that it had been a long time since he had been with a woman.

Shaking her head, she said, "I'll be sure to look both ways. Have a good night." She disappeared into the tavern.

He lingered a few more moments and watched her move through the tavern picking up stray glasses and plates.

Gannon started to whistle. As he turned to get his bike, he noticed his mailbox on the wall by his front door was full. He reached inside the rectan-

gular box and pulled out two days' worth of mail.
Most of it was junk flyers and bills.

Standing under the porch light, he started to flip
through the mail. He was halfway through the
stack when a packet of matches fell out of the stack
to the ground. The packet was red with lettering
embossed in gold.

Little Rome—Great Italian Food.

His blood ran cold.

The matches were identical to the ones Nero had
sent him after each Washington, D.C., fire.

He opened the pack. Inside was scrawled Day
One.

He closed his eyes, then quickly opened them
to refocus on the note. For a moment he couldn't
breathe. This was how it had begun with Nero in
D.C. a year and a half ago.

Gannon exhaled, tipping his face to the stars.
Anyone could have sent the matches. He'd made
no secret of his past when he'd moved to Preston
Springs and a good many knew he'd investigated
the Nero fires in D.C. The matches were common
knowledge, thanks to the Channel Five reporter,
Stephen Glass.

He glanced down at the matches. If this was someone's idea of a joke, it wasn't funny.

Sick bastard.

Pinching the bridge of his nose, he sighed, trying to release the tension from his shoulders. He was twisting himself up in knots.

One fire. One pack of matches. Neither countered the mountains of evidence the D.C. fire investigators found that proved the body in that warehouse was Nero.

Raymond Clyde Mason had been Nero's real name. The man who had terrorized D.C. for nearly a year was dead. Mason hadn't fit his idea of Nero, but gut reactions didn't hold a candle to the hard evidence that said Nero was dead. And whatever lingering doubts Gannon had had faded when the fires had stopped completely.

So why did he have the feeling that Nero was back?

"You're losing your mind, Gannon," he whispered.

Someone is jerking your chain.

Nero is dead.

He walked over to the trash can by the door and was ready to toss the matches away when he changed his mind and slipped them into his pocket.

Chapter 4

"Motorcycle Man, you are a pain," Darcy said, smiling as she stacked the dirty glasses on her tray.

Times were tough if she was semi-flirting with a redneck biker. Still, when she heard the roar of his bike engine, she moved to the window and watched him drive off into the night.

"What are you staring at?" Trevor shouted from behind the bar.

"Nothing." Turning from the window, she flipped the sign on the door to Closed and turned the lock. She wondered where Motorcycle Man would be riding to at this time of night. She started to run through possible scenarios when she caught herself. Who was she kidding? She'd come to Preston Springs to find Gannon and get a lead on Nero. Not for a fling.

Darcy moved to the bar where her brother was wiping up a spill. Trevor had lost his bright smile from earlier in the evening. Dark smudges hung under sunken eyes and judging by the way he moved, he was working on a headache. "Hey, Dee, do me a favor and finish closing up the bar."

She sat on a stool, groaning with pleasure to be off her feet. The counter behind the bar was littered with olives, limes and covered in a mixture of alcohols and juices. "I don't want to do it and you seem to be doing a good job of it."

He seemed agitated. "I've got to close out the register."

"Where's Mom?" Lord, but her back and legs ached. Hard to believe she held this job through high school and college.

Trevor went to the cash register, positioned a few feet to the right of the bar and directly in front of the door. He opened the register and scooped out all the money. "I sent her upstairs. She was wiped."

Darcy rubbed the back of her neck. Closing the

bar would take another hour and she could barely see straight as it was. This certainly wasn't what she'd pictured when she'd imagined her return home. "This sucks."

He laughed. "Hey, you wanted the job. I didn't come begging."

Imagining the Pulitzer in hand, Darcy stood. She moved behind the bar, punching him in the arm as she passed. She grabbed a rag. "Don't forget my check."

Rubbing his arm, he nudged her to the side sending her slightly off balance. "First thing in the morning."

She couldn't help but smile. "You're a real jerk."

He closed the register drawer. "Yeah, I love you, too."

"Hey, thanks."

He didn't look up from the cash in his hands. "For what?"

Tender emotions weren't her strong suit. "For letting me come back to work. It won't be for long. I swear."

His blue eyes softened. "You'd do the same for

me." He shoved the money into a bank deposit bag. "If you wipe down the bar, I'll sweep up."

"Bless you."

The instant Trevor left for the night deposit box, Darcy realized she'd gotten the short end of the stick. The bar was a real mess. She could have left it until the morning, but she pulled her own weight. She went to the small sink at the end of the bar, soaked the rag and started to clean.

A half hour later, Trevor returned from the bank. "I'm back." He looked alert and he'd lost the edginess.

Darcy wrung the rag out in the sink. "Good, you can sweep the floor."

He came into the bar. "I will. Hey, the bar looks good."

She lifted a brow—amazed at his energy. "Trevor you are the sloppiest bartender I ever met."

He shrugged good-naturedly. "Yeah, but no one makes a Gin Gimlet like I do."

No doubt it was a crusher. "So, get to sweeping."

"If you don't mind, I need to do a little inventory in the kitchen and then I'll come back and do it."

Darcy started to mop down the top of the bar. "You're slacking, Trev."

He lifted his elbows as she wiped past him. "Hey, I'm a man of my word."

God, she was tired. "Fine go, but I'm not sweeping."

Twenty minutes later, she'd finished cleaning. Her body aching, she started toward the back stairs ready to dive into her bed. She noticed Trevor's light was on in his office, but she didn't bother to check in with him. Each leg felt as if it weighed a hundred pounds as she climbed the darkened staircase. She made an effort to move quietly. Her mother had dog ears and she didn't want to wake her.

Two steps past her mother's door and she heard, "Darcy, have you checked to see if the front and back doors are locked?"

"I did the front. Trevor will get the back, Mom."

"Remind him."

If she'd had the strength, she'd have argued. But the end result would have been the same. She'd have to check the door. "Okay."

Turning, she flipped on the staircase light and

headed back downstairs. As she crossed the empty tavern room, she heard the roar of a motorcycle engine.

Darcy moved to the front tavern window and watched as Motorcycle Man pulled up in front of his garage. She paused and watched as he parked his bike under the streetlight and swung his leg over the side. Pulling off his helmet, he walked to the garage door and pulled it open. He flipped on the light.

There was an arrogance about his gait that reminded her of men in the military or the police force. She'd interviewed enough like that to recognize the look. But his longish hair and scraggly jeans and T-shirt screamed anti-establishment.

"So who are you, Motorcycle Man, and what brings you to this small town?" Her reporter's mind started to click. Without even realizing it, she'd ticked through a half dozen scenarios for him and had come up with the questions she'd ask if she had the chance to interview him. Hometown? Service record? Reason for leaving your last job? Why the interest in motorcycles?

Of course, she'd never interview him. His story,

despite his action hero swagger, wasn't likely the kind that grabbed headlines. She was after the big game—Nero.

Motorcycle Man tossed back his head, clearing his dark hair from his eyes, and pushed his bike into the garage. She watched as he stretched his long, lean body and reached for the garage door handle. He glanced toward the Varsity and for a minute she thought he was looking right at her. Her heart pounded in her chest. But, of course, he couldn't see her in the dark.

When he closed the door, she released the breath she'd been holding. He turned off the garage light.

Disappointment flickered. She liked looking at Motorcycle Man and wondered what he'd taste like if she kissed him. Darcy was acutely aware that there'd been no one in her bed since she and Stephen had broken up ten months ago. She missed the touch and feel of a man inside her.

But sex wasn't a casual thing for her. It required trust, and mustering trust had been hard since Stephen. She'd been taken in by his megawatt smile and handy excuses.

Motorcycle Man. He looked like he'd been

plucked out of *Easy Rider.* Clearly her judgment in men had not improved.

She turned from the window, moved to the door and checked the lock. It was secure. The grit from a night's worth of customers crunched under her feet and she realized Trevor had not swept yet. She went into the kitchen and noticed her brother's light was off. He'd left. She checked the back door. Unlocked.

Surprised that Trevor would have missed such an important detail, she turned the dead bolt. What the heck was the matter with him? Dad had always drilled security into their brains.

Trevor was getting sloppy.

Darcy woke at 6:00 a.m. She sat up and pushed her hair out of her eyes. She glanced around the room and for a moment didn't know where she was. Nothing seemed familiar to her. She blinked. Recognition dawned.

She rolled over and buried her head under the pillow. She dearly would have loved to sleep in another couple of hours but the Nero story wasn't going to write itself.

Darcy got out of bed and stretched. After hitting the bathroom, she went to the small dresser drawers, dug out her shorts and T-shirt and put on her jogging shoes.

A run was what she needed. She would get out in the fresh air, blow the cobwebs from her head and burn some of the calories she'd consumed last night. This last year since beginning her weight loss quest, she'd started running for the exercise because it was quick and effective. At first she'd hated it, but as she grew accustomed to the workouts, running became her best thinking time.

Then, after she'd showered, she'd find Gannon.

She pulled back her thick hair into a ponytail and headed down the staircase. The tavern was quiet. The chairs had been stacked on the tables but the floor hadn't been swept.

"Thanks, Trevor," she muttered as the faint smell of beer and cigarettes filled her nose.

Her stomach turned as she moved toward the kitchen and the coffeepot. She dumped yesterday's grounds down the disposal, scooped out fresh coffee and dropped in the filter. She filled the machine with water and flicked on the switch.

As the machine hissed, she leaned against the counter and stared at the kitchen. Her father had been an early riser and they'd often bumped into each other in the kitchen in the mornings. And they'd always managed to find something to fight about.

Darcy rubbed the tense muscles in the back of her neck with her hand. She could look back now and see that she'd started her share of the fights. She'd felt trapped in those days and could be a real bitch. If she'd had a little maturity, she'd have seen the old man was stressed out about the tavern finances. Throw in a roaring hangover, which he suffered almost daily, and you had an explosive mix.

She couldn't forgive the drinking but she could have diffused a lot of the tension. Instead she'd stirred it up.

Darcy heard her mother starting to move upstairs. The idea of facing her mother over coffee didn't appeal. She'd already dredged up enough memories for one day, so she headed out the back door to the alley and followed it to the street. She paused and stretched out the muscles in her legs and then started to run her old route.

Her muscles were tight and stiff as she started to jog down the sidewalk along Main Street, past the shops. By the time she reached the top of the hill, her legs started to relax and her gait fell into a steady pace. A fine sheen of sweat broke out on her forehead.

Her mind started to clear and her spirits lifted as the endorphins kicked in.

Her first night hadn't been very productive story-wise, but she'd gotten herself established and that was a good thing. It wouldn't take long to find Gannon in a town this small.

She jogged up a hill and her muscles groaned, demanding her attention. Breathing in slowly, she let the oxygen fill her lungs and nourish her muscles. The morning was warming up and she began to really sweat.

One of her first priorities was to get her money from Trevor. Her car's gas tank was on vapors, her credit card was maxed and she needed pocket money. No doubt Trevor was still sleeping but she'd catch up with him today. And when she did get her money, she would be mobile again.

Until then she was stuck.

As she headed down the hill, she heard the distant sound of sirens. She stopped, and wiping the sweat from her forehead, listened, trying to pinpoint the location. At first she thought they were police sirens but realized they belonged to fire trucks. Judging by the sounds, several trucks were headed out.

Another fire.

The sirens grew louder, coming from the north end of town. She started to run down the hill toward the warehouses. As she rounded a corner, she saw a large black plume of smoke rising up into bright blue morning sky.

Darcy ran toward the smoke and the sirens, which grew louder by the second. She hurried down the brick sidewalk and rounded the corner. She stopped immediately, coming face to face with the city's two fire trucks parked in front of Snead's Restaurant, which was engulfed in flames.

Snead's had once been an old tobacco warehouse. Three stories high, the owners had converted it two years ago. Darcy had kept up with local news through the Internet and had read that the Snead's restoration had cost over two hundred thousand dollars. It was set to open this weekend.

Through the windows she could see flames burning on all three floors. The fire had spread to the ceiling and had wrapped around the walls and door. The heat had shattered the glass, and smoke had blackened the red brick exterior.

The police had set up their cars as a barrier between the firefighters, and the policemen watched the growing crowd of onlookers.

She recognized the chief who watched as his captain dressed in his heavy fire gear and ordered crews to get in position with their hoses. Within minutes, a steady stream of water blasted the inferno. The fire hissed and spit. And the heavy scent of smoke saturated the air.

Darcy hung back, wrapping her arms around her chest. The heat was so intense that none of the firefighters approached the building. They continued to battle the blaze, but the building started to groan under the fire's attack. Timbers snapped and gave way inside. She winced and took a step back. The blaze had a life of its own.

Soon, it became clear the firefighters weren't

going to be able to save Snead's. Their priority shifted to saving the surrounding buildings. Most were historic and ripe for a stray flame or ember.

The intensity of this fire was so much like one of Nero's.

Darcy surveyed the crowd, knowing arsonists lingered so they could watch their fires. To her surprise, Motorcycle Man stood in the front row. He wore dark glasses. His hands in his pockets, he was simply dressed in faded jeans and a black T-shirt. His long dark hair skimmed his shoulders.

Even a quick glance would have told her he was more than a curiosity seeker. The force of his gaze was anything but casual. He took off his glasses and stared at the fire as if he were trying to read it, to communicate with it.

Very weird.

She shuddered. The guy definitely had issues.

Suddenly, Motorcycle Man shifted his gaze from the fire to her. The intensity sent tremors over her skin. For a moment she was thrown off, and then she took a good look at his face for the first time. In the light of day, she recognized him instantly.

Darcy took a step back and released a long, shuddering breath. *Michael Gannon*. The man she'd come to find had been right under her nose since she'd arrived in town. The man who was key to her story. And she'd flipped him the bird.

Color rose in her cheeks and she turned toward the fire. Her mind tripped and stumbled as she struggled to come up with something to say to him. Normally, she was good with opening lines but she couldn't scrape two coherent thoughts together. Worried that she'd miss her opportunity, she turned back to face him. She needed to make contact with him.

However, he'd vanished into the crowd.

She searched the group of people, scanning the sea of faces. But there was no sign of him.

Darcy heard the chief shout an order. As he returned to his truck, she ducked under the yellow police tape. She dashed up to him.

"Chief! What happened?"

He rubbed the back of his neck with a damp cloth. "Darcy, you need to get behind the lines."

She didn't move an inch. "I will. But what happened?"

He started to speak and then stopped. "I'm not talking to the press, Darcy."

"I'm officially an out-of-work reporter. Your secrets are safe with me." The lie didn't set well but for now she needed to stick to her cover.

He studied her an extra beat. "Honestly, we don't know. The place had just been okayed by the fire inspector in our department. Snead's was ready to open for business this weekend."

She felt naked without her pad and pencil. "Who called it in?"

"The owner. He was working on the back loading dock with a handful of employees. He smelled smoke and ordered everyone out of the building. Good thing, because ten minutes later the place was an inferno."

"Wouldn't the sprinkler system have put out any blaze?"

"It should have, but it didn't. It's as if the fire had a mind of its own. It's taking everything we have to contain it." He glanced back toward his men. "I've got to run Darcy. I'll catch up with you tonight."

She'd never seen the chief this rattled. "Sure."

Her mind started to turn. A fast moving blaze

and an ineffective sprinkler system. Either the sprinklers had been faulty or something or someone had accelerated the fire.

Gannon. Nero. The two new fires. The three combined was just too much of a coincidence.

Nero stood away from the crowd, careful to stay out of the line of sight of the police. There was the off chance someone was videotaping the crowd. Except for Gannon, it was unlikely anyone suspected him. But he had to be careful in case someone had connected the two fires.

He should have stayed away altogether, but he loved to watch his fires dance. They were his children.

And today, his fire moved magnificently, burning hotter and higher than he'd expected. The proud tall building was crumbling so quickly to ashes.

Almost *too* quickly.

He liked to savor his fires, drinking in the fear of the crowds, the panic in the firefighters' voices and, of course, Gannon's reaction. He made a note to use less accelerant next time. Hadn't he learned patience and being in the moment from yoga?

Exhilaration singed his veins as he casually strode away from the decimated restaurant. He got into his car and drove back into town.

He reached for the front door of the post office at the same time a mother and her infant did. The kid was about a year old, grinning up at him with his three teeth.

Cute. Nero smiled back at the child. He held the door open for the young mother and then followed her inside.

He moved off to the side where there was counter space for addressing letters. He addressed and stamped a plain white envelope to Michael Gannon. For a moment, he felt a twinge of regret. When he'd sworn off fires a year ago, he'd meant it. He didn't want the hassle of the chase anymore. He wanted peace from this maddening compulsion to see the world burn.

For many months, he thought he'd kicked the habit. But, in late spring, the urges returned. He'd fought them for a time, focusing on yoga and re-laxation. But, he discovered that peace was highly overrated. He missed the excitement, the thrill and the need to see his beauties sway. So he'd started to set small fires. Nothing major. Abandoned buildings and brush fires mostly.

But without Gannon, the fun was simply not there. The fear of being caught by him made sinning that much edgier, sweeter.

So, he'd come to Gannon, which hadn't been hard because he'd kept track of the arson investigator since Gannon had left D.C.

Nero had to admire Gannon. The man was getting on with his life. His garage was doing reasonably well and no doubt once his bikes hit the circuit, he would become very well known.

Yes, Gannon was a worthy opponent. He was going to make the game fun.

Nero slipped his hand into his pocket and pulled out a pack of *Rome* matches. The coated stock of the cover felt slick and smooth to the touch. On the inside flap, he wrote, "The game has begun again."

He tucked the matches into the envelope and sealed it. Whistling, he dropped it into the box.

Chapter 5

Darcy sprinted back to the tavern. Her heart pumped and her muscles sang. She hadn't felt this energized in weeks. Today's fire was eerily similar to the D.C. fires, and she knew Nero—or a very savvy copycat—was at work.

The trick now was discovering the arsonist's identity.

Wiping the sweat from her eyes, she entered the Varsity kitchen's back door. The room was quiet and the coffeepot empty, a sign her mother had come and gone.

Grateful she didn't have to face her mother, she paced the kitchen, restless. If she cracked this story, the exposure would be sensational. Her name would finally be on everyone's radar screen. Oh, and the look on Stephen's face. Priceless.

"Stop," she warned herself. "You're getting ahead of yourself."

Now, it was more important than ever to talk to Gannon. He was the key to Nero and the fires. Somehow, the two were irrevocably linked.

Darcy took the back stairs two at a time, dashed into her room and kicked the door closed. She tugged off her running shoes and stripped off her clothes, leaving everything in a heap on the floor. Humming, she turned on the shower and hopped into the stall.

The shower's cold water shocked her senses and she let out a whoop. But she stood under the icy spray, letting it cool her hot skin. For a moment, she turned her face into the water and let the water cascade over her body. Her heart hammered. When her skin cooled, she turned the water to warm, sighing as her muscles relaxed. She lathered soap in her hand and started to rub the sweat from her body.

Her thoughts turned to Gannon again. At the

fire, he'd stared at her with an animal awareness that was very primitive and alluring. It was clear he was attracted to her. Even now, she could feel the stark intensity of his gaze.

Her ex-fiancé's lovemaking had always been very civilized. Lights off, under the blankets. It had been good but never satisfying, not on a primal level.

Darcy didn't imagine that Gannon was civilized in the bedroom. If he walked into her bathroom right now, he'd have no qualms about taking her where she stood. Her heart beat faster. She pictured him stepping into the stall, naked, the water beading on his broad, muscled chest. He'd run his large, rough hands over her belly and cup her breasts.

Warmth blossomed deep in her core and quickly spread through her body. What did Gannon's lips taste like? What would his calloused hands feel like against her naked skin?

She turned off the water. "This is nuts." She grabbed a towel and started to dry herself off. "I don't mix business with pleasure."

She wrapped the towel around her wet hair and walked into her bedroom. Digging clothes out of her suitcase, she got dressed in well-worn jeans and a red T-shirt. She blew her hair dry, put on mascara, blush and a little lipstick.

Darcy went down to the kitchen and brewed herself another cup of coffee. Still no sign of her mother or Trevor. She dug out a slice of cheese and a piece of ham from the fridge. Wrapping the ham around the cheese, she leaned against the counter and bit into the roll.

She would have to move carefully with Gannon. He hated reporters. But before she could tackle Gannon, she needed her money.

As she finished her meal, she found herself staring at the door to Trevor's office, located off the kitchen. She took a step toward it and then stopped. It was one thing to snoop for a living, quite another to snoop on your own family.

Curiosity quickly got the better of her, and she crossed to the office door and turned the handle. It was unlocked. What would a tiny peek hurt? She opened the door, half expecting to see Trevor sitting where her father had for so many years.

But Trevor wasn't there. And to her surprise, the office was a wreck. The desk, which pushed against the wall and faced away from the door, was piled high with stacks of unopened mail. Newspapers littered the floor.

"God, if Dad were alive, he'd have a fit," she muttered as she made her way through the mess. Her father had always run a tight ship. He might have been out of control in his personal life, but he always craved order in his business.

She sat down in the desk's wooden swivel chair and pushed aside a stack of bills so she could set down her cup of coffee.

Darcy felt another twinge of guilt for snooping but Trevor had her money. And technically speaking, she did have a stake in the business. Her father had left her a one-third share in the tavern, a fact that surprised everyone including her. Of course, the other two-thirds had gone to her mother and Trevor. And until now, Darcy had been happy to leave the business to them.

As she started to sift through the papers, she noticed the laptop underneath. By the looks of it, it was state of the art, brand new. Maybe Trevor wasn't such a wreck after all. Maybe he stayed organized on the computer.

She opened the laptop and turned on the power

button. When the desktop came up, she sorted through the unopened bank statements. She opened the most recent she could find—two months old—and read it. According to the statement, the tavern was in decent financial shape. The statement referenced the online account, so she pulled up the bank's Web site. She typed in the account number, and to her relief, the computer automatically supplied the password.

Darcy wasn't expecting to find a ton of money, but she imagined there'd be enough to cover her loan. The account contained fifty dollars.

"This has to be a mistake," she said. "There's got to be more money somewhere."

Her elbow bumped a stack of envelopes piled high by the computer and they slid onto the keyboard. They were unpaid bills—the utility company, the water company, trash collection and the produce man she'd paid yesterday. She opened one after the other. Each had PAST DUE stamped in red.

If these bills were any indication, the Varsity was in big financial trouble. "None of this makes sense," she said. Last night, business had been booming, no doubt thanks to George's good cooking. And it had been a Tuesday, typically one of their slow nights. A good weekend could pull in enough to cover all these bills plus more.

So where was the money going?

The kitchen back door opened and closed with a bang and Darcy rose from the desk and went into the kitchen.

Her mother glanced up at her as she set a crate of apples on the kitchen counter. "What were you doing in Trevor's office?"

Unrepentant, she shrugged. "Looking through the tavern accounts."

Mrs. Sampson's face flushed with anger. "You have no right to do that. Trevor is the manager of the Varsity."

"He's not doing a very good job of it judging from what I just saw."

Her mother set the crate down hard on the floor. Blue eyes flashed with fury. "How dare you judge? Trevor works very hard."

If Darcy had a lick of sense, she'd back off. Get her money and get out. How Trevor led his life was none of her business. But for some reason, she couldn't let it go. "He didn't look like he was breaking much of a sweat last night."

Mrs. Sampson shook her head and raised her hand, both signs that she didn't want to hear what Darcy had to say. "You don't know anything about anything." She walked to the sink and started to fill it with water.

Darcy hated the way her mother ignored problems. She'd been a master at pretending that her marriage wasn't a disaster and that her husband wasn't a verbally abusive alcoholic. Darcy had learned from a young age to stay clear of her old man when the Johnnie Walker bottle appeared.

Determined to stay civil, she kept her voice soft. "I know trouble when I see it, Mom. Something is going on with Trevor."

Her mother slammed down her hands on the counter. "Darcy, I'm sick of you always stirring things up. If there ever was trouble in this house, you were always at the root of it. I'd hoped you'd outgrown that annoying habit."

The accusation slashed through the heart of old insecurities. "I was the only one willing to talk about the fact that Dad was an alcoholic."

Tears pooled in her mother's eyes. "Your father was a fine, decent man."

"When he was sober." She shoved out a breath. "Everyone pegged me as the troublemaker in the family, but counseling this past year has taught me that I was only a symptom of our dysfunctional family."

Her mother's face flushed with anger. "We are not dysfunctional. And I resent you for saying that."

Darcy was treading on dangerous ground with her mother and decided to back up a step. "Hey, I don't want Trevor to be in trouble. I hope for all our sakes he's got money squirreled away somewhere. I hope what I saw on his computer was wrong. Because if it's not, we are all in deep trouble."

Her mother's back was rigid. "Trevor is taking care of everything—just like your father used to."

A heavy sadness overwhelmed Darcy. She realized, then, that she'd never reach her mother. The woman lived in her own world and there was no changing it. Darcy would always be the outsider in her family no matter how many articles she wrote or how many awards she won.

Suddenly, she couldn't breathe. "Believe what you want to believe, Mom. I'm not going to argue anymore." Savagely, she brushed a tear from her cheek. "I've got to get out of here."

Her mother lifted her chin. "Don't come back until you have a better attitude."

Darcy stormed out into the alley, her blood throbbing in her temples. She'd been a fool to think she could have talked to her mother. "Damn."

As she headed down the uneven sidewalk curving down Main Street past the other shops, she reached in her pocket and pulled out a twenty-dollar bill. Add this to her bank balance and she had all of two hundred and twenty dollars to her name.

Too shaky to interview Gannon or anyone else for that matter, she decided to duck into the coffee shop across the street. She glanced both ways, waited for two cars to pass and then dashed toward the coffee shop.

The bells on the door over her head jingled as she pushed through the front door of the coffee shop. Scents of cinnamon and coffee greeted her. The shop was long and narrow. In front of an exposed brick wall stood a counter with an antique cash register and a glistening pastry display case filled with goodies. Across the room, six round tables surrounded by wooden chairs sat clustered together. Half were full of customers sipping coffee. The dim lights and chilled air reminded her of a winter afternoon, the perfect time for coffee.

She took a couple of deep breaths to soothe the tension in her back before heading to the front counter where a young kid with blue spiked hair and a nose ring stood.

The kid grinned. "Can I help you?"

"Soy cappuccino," she said.

"Sure thing," he said. "Can I get you a pastry today?"

This last year she'd trained herself to stay away from sweets. But today she wasn't worried about calories, fat grams or carbohydrates. She needed comfort food. "Throw in two sugar cookies, as well."

The young man grinned. "Coming up."

The coffee and cookies set her back five dollars and twenty cents. At these prices, this would be her last splurge for a while. Shoving her precious change into her pocket, Darcy headed to the side bar where she dumped the blue sweetener into her coffee.

"So is that the breakfast of champions?" Nathan's deep voice had her turning.

His light hair hung recklessly in his eyes and his bright green eyes twinkled. He wore a crisp button-down shirt, khakis and loafers without socks. He looked so neat, clean and composed.

Despite her morning, she grinned. "Sugar, fat, artificial sweeteners and caffeine are the four major food groups, aren't they?"

His laugh was deep and rich. "Oh, that's right. I keep forgetting." He glanced toward the clerk, then back at her. "I'm getting some coffee. Can I join you? I'm waiting on a friend but could use the company until he arrives."

"That would be great. I'll get us a table."

He winked. "Be right there."

Charmed, Darcy selected a small round table in the corner. A few minutes later, Nathan joined her with his steaming latte. "I stop in here every day. They've got the best coffee outside of New York."

"Are you from New York?" Idle chat suited her just fine for the moment.

"It was one stop along the way." He sipped his coffee. "I've lived all over."

"And you were born and raised in the heart of Virginia?"

"Guilty. Even went to college twenty miles away in Roanoke." He sipped his coffee. "Did I see you running this morning?"

"I run just about every day." It felt good to talk about regular things.

Nathan looked like a man who was comfortable in his own skin. "How far do you run?"

"Four miles."

"Fair distance."

"Normally, it's farther. My run got cut a little short today by the fire."

His face hardened a fraction. "I just heard about the fire. Terrible."

"Did you see it?"

"No. I was up early this morning on a conference call with my boss. We'll be putting up steel at the site starting this week and there were figures to discuss." He sipped his coffee. "I hear the restaurant was a complete loss."

"I didn't think a building could be destroyed so fast." She bit into her cookie, savoring the buttery taste.

"Do you know if the owner had insurance?"

"I don't." The bells on the café door jingled and, on reflex, she looked up. Whatever else she'd planned to say to Nathan vanished from her head. Michael Gannon strode into the café.

Gannon glanced in her direction. His intense gaze captured hers and for a moment she felt a deep connection to him. She remembered the way he'd looked at her at the fire and the fantasies she'd had about him in the shower.

Then his gaze shifted to Nathan and all traces of emotion vanished before he turned toward the counter and placed his order.

"Coffee. Black." His rusty voice sent tingles down her spine.

A hint of warmth rose in her cheeks. She took a bite of her cookie. How was she supposed to not only act cool but also find a way to pick his brain about Nero?

"So you know Gannon?" Nathan said following her line of sight.

"What? Oh no, not really. I've just seen him around town."

Nathan stood up as Gannon approached with his coffee. "What took you so long?"

Darcy glanced between Nathan and Gannon. This was the *friend* he'd been expecting. Great. Just great. Setting down her cookie, she brushed the crumbs from her lap and summoned her best interview smile. This chance meeting could work to her advantage if she kept it together.

Nathan placed his hand gently on her shoulder. "Darcy Sampson, I'd like you to meet my friend, Michael Gannon. We met in D.C. last year when I was doing a project out in Loudoun County. He moved to Preston Springs about eleven months ago and now owns the motorcycle shop across the street from the Varsity."

"Oh," she said, standing. "Right."

"Gannon, this is Darcy Sampson. Her family owns the Varsity and she is native to Preston Springs."

Gannon nodded. "Darcy."

Her name sounded different when Gannon said it. It sounded smoky—seductive.

"Gannon would stay holed up in that bike shop of his for days if I didn't drag him out for coffee occasionally," Nathan said.

"Right." A half smile tipped the edge of Gannon's lips.

She suspected he accepted these coffee breaks more out of kindness than any need to be around people. Born in another time, Gannon would have been a mountain man.

She still couldn't get over the fact that this guy was Michael Gannon. He didn't look anything like he had a year ago. The hair was no longer military short but swept the top of his shoulders. He'd swapped suits for a biker T-shirt and jeans. His entire aura had changed.

Darcy struggled to speak coherently. "I almost didn't recognize you without the motorcycle and helmet."

The corner of Gannon's mouth rose further. "I almost didn't recognize you without the trash can."

"Did I miss something here?" Nathan asked. He pulled out her seat and the trio sat down.

Darcy cleared her throat. "Mr. Gannon and I met accidentally in the alley yesterday."

Gannon sipped his coffee. "I nearly ran her over with my bike and she shot me the bird."

Darcy's face flushed with heat. "Sorry. Not one of my better days."

Nathan chuckled. "I've known Gannon a couple of years. He always did bring out the best in women."

Gannon's eyes flashed with amusement. "It's a talent."

Darcy cleared her throat. "What brought you to Preston Springs, Mr. Gannon?"

"It's just Gannon. And I liked the scenery," he said.

"It's beautiful country here," she said.

Inwardly she groaned. What did she want to talk about next—the weather? She sat here with the man who knew Nero better than anyone and she couldn't think of an intelligent thing to say. She was grateful when Nathan started talking to Gannon about interest rates and property values.

Her mind drifted back to that time when the fires had gripped Washington. She, like everyone else in town, had been so relieved when Stephen reported that Nero had died in his last fire. The whole city had been thrilled. Gannon had disappeared from the scene altogether after the fires ended.

And now Gannon was in Preston Springs and the fires had started here.

She sipped her coffee. It tasted bitter.

The image of Gannon standing at today's fire flashed in her head. When his gaze had shifted to her, she'd assumed the raw, sexual intensity had been directed at her. But what if his passion hadn't been for her? What if it was the fire that had turned him on?

Gannon had been pegged a hero in D.C. but what if he was no hero at all?

What if he was Nero?

Damn.

The idea was stunning—shattering. If she could prove one of the nation's top arson investigators was in fact a serial arsonist who had killed twelve people, she could write her own ticket.

Her heart was pounding so loudly in her ears, she feared the whole café could hear it.

To calm her racing heart, she reviewed the facts.

One. Gannon had been at the fire today.

Two. He'd been watching with a fanatic intensity.

Three. Arsonists loved to watch their fires burn.

"Darcy?" Nathan said. "Where'd you go?"

Her attention snapped back. "Sorry. Just drifted for a moment."

"Did we bore you with our talk of buildings and mortgages?" Nathan said.

"No, it was fascinating," she said.

Gannon chuckled. "Right."

Nathan adjusted his glasses. "I was wondering if you'd like to come out and see the condos."

"Oh, yeah, sure. That would be great." She didn't care about the development but accepting the offer seemed the right thing to do.

Gannon tapped his finger on the side of his coffee cup. "So what brings you to Preston Springs, Darcy?"

She hesitated. "I'm in between jobs so I figured I'd drive back and take it easy for a while. My family owns the Varsity and since they were short-handed, they offered me a job."

"They were working you pretty hard last night in the tavern," Nathan said.

She could feel Gannon's gaze on her. "I don't mind the work. Keeps me off the streets," she joked.

Nathan laughed.

Gannon didn't.

"So you own the garage, Gannon?" she said scrambling for more questions. "When I was a kid, the guy who owned it specialized in fixing Ford trucks. He called it American Parts."

"I figured as much by the stacks of old Ford manuals," Gannon said.

Nervous she tried not to squirm in her seat. If Gannon was Nero, this would be the biggest story of the decade. *Pulitzer. Pulitzer. Pulitzer.* "That was some fire." Brilliant transition. Hitting Gannon over the head would have been less subtle.

Gannon didn't respond. He tapped his long finger on the side of his coffee cup.

However, Nathan was eager to pick up the thread of the conversation. "Sounds like I missed a real show."

It surprised her that Gannon didn't want to talk

about the fire. She figured a true arsonist savored the damage he created. "I spoke to the chief after it was all over," she said, trying not to look at Gannon too much. "He's been a regular at the tavern for years. Anyway, he said the fire was one of the most intense he'd ever seen." She hesitated. "You were there weren't you, Gannon?"

Gannon traced the rim of his cup with a calloused finger. "Yeah, I saw the smoke and came running."

"What did you think?" she said, trying to keep her voice neutral.

"A helluva mess, like you said." Gannon didn't elaborate.

"Was anyone hurt?" Nathan asked.

"No," Gannon replied.

"Thank God," Nathan muttered as he sipped his coffee.

Getting information out of Gannon was like squeezing blood from a stone. "I heard the guys in the bar talking about another fire," Darcy said. "What was it that burned down?"

"A Super 8," Nathan said.

"You think they are related?" she asked.

Nathan shrugged. "Who's to say? But I wouldn't be surprised. Maybe Larry is right. Could be teen gangs."

"What do you think, Gannon?" A small white scar ran along the edge of his jaw from his ear to his mouth. She wondered where he'd gotten it.

Gannon looked down at his cup. He took a sip. He clearly didn't like talking about the fires. "Can't say."

"I'll bet it's the talk of the tavern tonight," she added, hoping he'd snag the bait.

Instead, Gannon rose. "Nathan, Darcy, I've got to run. I just remembered I've got a supplier stopping by the shop in a couple of minutes."

Nathan smiled easily. "Oh yeah, sure. We'll catch up soon."

Darcy stood, trying to hide her disappointment. "It was nice to meet you—officially."

Gannon nodded. "Yeah."

After Gannon had left she and Nathan made small talk, though she found it hard to concentrate on anything but Nero. While she drank her coffee and ate the cookies, she itched to follow

Gannon and ask him a hundred other questions on her mind.

The thought of breaking the Nero story made her giddy.

Some days, life could be so sweet.

Chapter 6

Gannon spent most of that night dreaming about Nero. The flames, the crazy puzzles, the victims— they all haunted him. At 5:00 a.m., he finally gave up on sleep and rose. He was exhausted and in a foul mood.

After he showered and drank a pot of coffee, he got into his car and drove to the fire department's main offices. He needed to talk with the fire chief. He wasn't expecting a warm reception. Not only was he an outsider, but he was also retired from a department far from this jurisdiction. Technically, the fires were none of his business.

But as he'd watched the fire burn yesterday, the

speed and the intensity of the blaze had all screamed Nero—or at least someone who thought he was Nero. Preston Springs—his town—had a serial arsonist in its midst.

He parked his car and strode through the glass front doors. He stopped at the receptionist's desk and asked to speak to the chief.

"He's in meetings," the older woman said, cupping her hand over a phone cradled on her shoulder.

"Chief Wheeler and I are friends," he lied. He knew the chief loved motorcycles because he had stopped by his shop a couple of times to check out his inventory. He'd never bought anything, but he liked dreaming. "We've been trying to hook up for days now. I've got a new motorcycle in I thought he might like to see. When will he be available?"

The woman's frown deepened as her gaze traveled over Gannon's faded jeans and worn T-shirt. "Sorry, but he really is tied up. I can have him give you a call."

He forced a smile. "Don't worry. I'll catch up with him."

Gannon started to leave and the receptionist returned to her call. But instead of heading outside, he turned and made a beeline around her desk toward the chief's office. The receptionist shouted for him to stop, but he didn't listen. He barged into the chief's office.

The chief sat at his desk, studying a thick file. He glanced up clearly annoyed and surprised by the interruption. Recognition softened his glare. "Gannon?"

"We need to talk."

"About? I'm up to my eyeballs in paperwork today."

The receptionist stumbled to a stop behind Gannon. "I tried to stop him, sir, but he just barged right past my desk."

Unapologetic, Gannon held his ground. "This is important, Chief. It's about the fires."

Chief Wheeler glanced at the receptionist. "Thanks, Sue. I'll take it from here." He waited until she'd left and closed the door before he motioned for Gannon to sit. "What about the fires?"

Gannon's body jumped with adrenaline. He wanted to pace but made himself sit. "I think you've got a serial arsonist in town."

The chief rubbed the back of his neck. "What makes you think that? We've had two fires in the last week, one of which can be explained away by faulty construction."

This bit of information surprised him. "You know the motel fire was construction related for certain?"

"Preliminary reports suggest it."

"The reports are wrong."

Chief Wheeler's eyes narrowed. "I'll admit we're not a big city department, but we're not rookies fresh from the academy either, Gannon."

Frustration rose in his throat. "I don't want this to turn into an ego thing, Chief. This is about stopping the fires."

Annoyance tightened the chief's jaw. "What makes you think there are going to be more fires?"

Gannon dug in his pocket for the packs of matches. "Someone sent me these."

The chief took the Rome matches and studied them. "Okay, matches."

"Open the flap."

The chief read the inscription. *Day One.*

"I got those yesterday. If Nero holds to his pattern, I'll get more matches today."

The chief lifted a brow. "Nero? Gannon, he's dead."

Gannon was certain now that the body found in that last D.C. fire was not Nero's. He had no facts—just a sick feeling in the pit of his stomach.

But convincing the chief and everyone else that Nero was alive was a different matter.

He decided for now to downplay Nero. "What I meant to say was I think you've got a Nero copycat on your hands."

"Why the devil would a copycat land in Preston Springs?"

"Because I'm here."

Chief Wheeler leaned back in his chair and folded his arms over his chest. "Seems a bit farfetched."

"I was Nero's target for seven months. It stands to reason a copycat would do the same."

"Look, I know life can seem pretty dull here compared to D.C."

"Look, I'm not some has-been investigator looking for trouble when there isn't any."

The chief raised an eyebrow. "Didn't say that

you were. But I can tell you that two fires and one pack of matches doesn't mean we got anything other than two unrelated fires. Maybe someone sent those matches to you as a joke."

Gannon flexed the tension from his fingers. "It's not a damn bit funny."

The chief was losing patience. "Didn't say it was."

"There's more to this, Chief, I can feel it."

"Feelings don't do much for me." The chief rose. "Tell you what. You go back to building those motorcycles, and I'll take care of the fire fighting."

Gannon stood so quickly his chair skidded back on the carpeted floor. "I don't need your condescending attitude, Chief. I came here to warn you that there could be more fires."

Anger flashed in the chief's gray eyes. "And I don't need you barging in my office when I got work to do. You get hard evidence and we'll talk."

Gannon was so mad he could hardly see straight. No one would blame him if he walked away. He'd more than paid his dues. Instead, he heard himself saying, "Watch the schools."

The comment caught the chief off guard. "Why?"

"If the pattern holds true, the Nero wannabe is going to torch a school next."

Chief Wheeler's lips flattened. "Don't jerk my chain, son."

"I'm not," he ground out. "Believe me, this is the last kind of situation I want to be in."

Gannon left the office angry and irritated. There were going to be more fires. Fires were a game to Nero and he'd clearly enjoyed the cat and mouse game they'd played in D.C.

He drove back to his garage and parked in the back alley. He tossed his keys on the workbench by the back door and headed straight to his tools. On the lift sat the bike he was supposed to finish and send to the paint shop next week. He'd spent most of yesterday fabricating the custom handlebars and now he needed to attach them to the bike.

Aggravated, he put on his welding mask and fired up his torch. The chief was a fool. He stared at the blue-white flame and found himself transported back to the fires that had ravaged the D.C.

area last year. He thought about the lives lost. The destruction. The fear.

Gannon forced his focus back to the bike. He started to weld metal to metal.

Nero, or some nut who thought he was, was out there just waiting to set more fires. Gannon had done his part and tried to warn the chief. It wasn't his fault that the guy wouldn't listen.

Watch the schools.

Gannon's own words haunted him. No matter how much he wanted to let this go, he couldn't. He shut off the torch. When he turned, he saw Darcy standing by the door.

The long-legged brunette was holding a stack of mail. A smile tipped the edge of her full lips.

She wore shorts and a white T-shirt. The one bright spot about last night had been the dream he'd had about her. She'd been naked. Willing. Hot. He'd taken her on this very workbench.

He set down the torch. "Can I help you?"

He fantasized about taking her upstairs right now and spending the better part of the day in bed with her. No love. No promises. Just hot sex.

"Look, I'm new in town," she said. "I mean I am

from Preston Springs, but I haven't been back in a year. Long story short, I don't know many people under the age of sixty anymore. I was thinking you'd like to have lunch with me."

That was about the last thing he expected. "Why?"

His question made her laugh. "I don't know, I thought it could be fun."

"Fun. It's been my experience that everybody does something for a reason."

She arched an eyebrow. "Fun isn't reason enough?"

"Not generally."

She didn't look offended. "Look, I'm just asking for a lunch date, not a trip down the aisle, sport. If you don't want to go out with me then just say so. I'm a big girl and can take it."

She had a spine. He liked that. That didn't mean that he didn't think she was up to something. She was. But what better way to find out her agenda than over lunch. "Lunch sounds good."

The slight tension in her face softened. She checked her watch. "It's just ten-thirty now. How about I pick you up at twelve?"

"Twelve is good. But I'll pick you up. And wear jeans. We'll go for a ride on my motorcycle. That is, if you aren't afraid of bikes."

She grinned. "There's little that frightens me."

This was going to be fun. "See you at twelve."

Darcy was terrified of motorcycles.

There was something about hurtling down the road—exposed—on a piece of metal that defied common sense.

But she'd be damned if a motorcycle ride was going to scare her off this date. So, she spent the next hour going over the questions she wanted to ask Gannon.

She had to be very careful. If Gannon was Nero, he was dangerous. And even if he was just the burned-out investigator, she still needed his help.

She settled on wearing a pink T-shirt, jeans and boots. And though she'd have denied it, she did spend extra time with her makeup and hair. In the end, she pulled her long curls into a high ponytail. The style was neat, efficient and didn't look like she'd tried as hard as she had. She hurried down the back stairs through the kitchen.

Her mother was at the stove, cutting onions for a pot of chili. "So where are you headed?"

"Lunch."

"A date?"

"Not exactly."

Her mother frowned. "The tavern hasn't been swept."

"Trevor said he'd do it."

"He's not here."

She refused to be drawn into an argument. "I'll be back by two. Time enough to sweep and get prepped for the dinner crowd." She opened the screened door. "Where is Trevor anyway?"

Her mother's shoulders stiffened. "I'm sure he'll be here any minute."

"Right. Well, when you see him, tell him I need to be paid back."

Her mother's jaw tightened. "He'll make good on your check."

"Let's hope so." She'd invited Gannon to lunch so by her way of thinking, she was on the hook for the bill. Her credit card, tucked in her back pocket, was almost maxed out but she could charge the meal if Gannon didn't go nuts when he ordered.

She crossed the room and kissed her mother on the cheek.

Her mother looked at her, surprise in her tired eyes. "What was that for?"

"Sorry about the fight earlier."

Her mother nodded stiffly. "Have a good lunch."

It was the closest her mother had ever come to an endearment. "See you in a couple of hours."

Darcy headed out the back door and walked to the front of the tavern. At exactly twelve noon, she heard the roar of a motorcycle engine as Gannon rounded the corner on his bike.

Her insides fluttered. God, but he looked so fine in his leather jacket and black helmet. Be cool, Sampson. Don't act like a blithering idiot just because the man wears leather.

He stopped in front of her and flipped open his visor. Again, his gaze traveled up and down her body. Heat rose through her body into her cheeks.

"Ready to go?" he asked.

"Absolutely."

He reached behind him and unhooked a spare helmet fastened to the seat. "Put this on."

Darcy tried to put her helmet on but realized

her high ponytail got in the way. Refusing to see this as a sign from above, she handed him back the helmet. "Sorry, too much hair. I'll need to re-adjust."

His grin reached his eyes this time. "Take your time."

She felt awkward as she pulled out the pony-tail she'd spent fifteen minutes smoothing out. With him watching, her fingers trembled slightly. Quickly, she repositioned her ponytail to the base of her neck and took the helmet back from him. This time it fit perfectly.

Hesitating just an instant, she swung her leg over the back of the bike. "What do I hold on to?"

He flipped his visor down. "Me. Just wrap your arms around my waist."

She scooted up behind him and wrapped her arms around his waist. Her breasts flattened against his hard back, all sinew and muscle. He didn't wear any cologne like Stephen had. He had a musky clean scent that she really liked.

"Have you ever been on a bike before?" he asked.

"No. This is my first time."

"I promise to be gentle."

Her laugh was deep and genuine. "Thanks."

Once she'd snapped her helmet strap, he revved the engine, checked for traffic and pulled out onto Main Street.

As he rounded his first turn and opened the bike up, Darcy immediately tensed. She felt vulnerable riding on the back of the bike with nothing to hold on to but Gannon. He seemed comfortable enough and he seemed to know what he was doing, but images of crashing into the pavement nagged her. She squeezed her eyes shut.

She wanted him to slow down but her pride balked. She'd hang on to him and enjoy this ride, or at least pretend to, even if it killed her.

Gannon, however, seemed unfazed by it all. His body was relaxed, yet she had the sense that he was firmly in control.

As the minutes clicked by, she started to relax and loosen the death grip she had on Gannon's waist. Cracking one lid open, she saw that they'd turned onto Route 250 and were heading west, higher into the mountains.

The trees were beautiful and the sky a vivid blue. The air rushing past them should have left her chilled, but the hot sun combined with the heat of Gannon's body left her feeling very comfortable.

Before she realized it, she was really enjoying herself.

Gannon drove another fifteen minutes. When he started to gear down, she looked up and saw a small roadside restaurant called Gully's. Darcy remembered Gully's from her high school days. A hangout for locals, the classic greasy spoon had the best burgers in the county. Just one story, the brick building had tiny windows and a small white front door. Most tourists didn't know of its reputation and drove right by, assuming it was an abandoned dive. Darcy remembered it also only took cash.

She had a moment of panic when she realized all she had was her Visa. Slick, Sampson, real slick. Invite a man to a business lunch and then hit him up for a loan.

Gannon parked the bike and shut off the engine. She glanced toward the small door. To her great relief she spotted the credit card stickers.

As Darcy swung her leg over the side and pulled off her helmet, she found she missed the thrill of the ride and the closeness of Gannon's body.

Keep it professional, Sampson. This is strictly business.

"Great ride," she said, sounding as excited as she felt.

He took her helmet and attached them both to the seat of the bike. "I thought you were going to bail on me at first. You were as tense as a wound rubber band."

Grinning, she brushed her bangs back into place. "I had my doubts at first. I was certain I was hurtling to my death."

He laughed, flashing even white teeth. "And you didn't bail? Takes guts."

"Not guts. Fear of humiliation."

He escorted her through the narrow front door into the dimly lit restaurant. It was just as she remembered. Twenty booths covered in red fake leather, walls painted a muddy white and a faded chrome jukebox in the corner. The place was packed. Only a couple of tables remained open.

"The place hasn't changed a bit," she said. "I wonder if they still serve the Mammoth burger."

Surprise flashed in his eyes. "So much for trying to impress you with my knowledge of *The Best Off-the-Road Eats.*"

"Oh, I am impressed. Usually only the natives and truckers know about Gully's."

A waitress motioned them toward an empty table. "Menus are on the table."

"Thanks," Gannon said. He guided her to an empty booth and they took their seats. "I stumbled onto the place by accident about six months ago."

She picked up a laminated menu from the table and glanced down at it. As she searched for their salads, she reminded herself that even psychopaths could be charming. "So how long have you been in town?"

He studied his menu. "About a year."

The third degree would not be cool, but she itched to ask him a million different questions. Instead, she backed off. "As I remember, the cheeseburgers are this side of heaven."

"I go for the dogs."

"Excellent choice."

A waitress wearing jeans and a red T-shirt gave them each a glass of ice water, took their order and menus. "Be back in a few minutes with your drinks."

Darcy sipped her water, trying her best to look

relaxed and confident. And confident she should be. Interviewing people was her thing. She'd grilled council members, the mayor and business leaders. A retired fire fighter/possible arsonist should be a piece of cake.

Then again, who was she kidding? There was nothing simple about Michael Gannon. She'd bet the guy had more layers than an onion. "So, where are you from, Gannon?" The question stumbled out of her mouth as if she were a rookie reporter. She sipped more water to cover.

"Washington, D.C."

"Hey, that's my old stomping grounds. What brings you this far afield?"

His steady gaze remained on her and didn't waver. "Change of pace. Got tired of the traffic."

"The traffic is a nightmare up there." Okay, we've covered hometown and traffic. Now, how was she going to transition that into *Hey, I'm a reporter trying to dig up dirt on Nero. Do you think he is alive and well? Or better, are you Nero?* Instead, she said, "It always takes me a few days to decompress when I head outside the Beltway."

"It took me about three months before I stopped

waking at 5:00 a.m., and dreading the commute in to work."

She noticed his strong wrists and long fingers. No grease under the nails. "You live close to work now?"

"Right above the garage."

"Sounds like my setup. I'm living above the tavern."

The waitress arrived with their drinks and promised to have their order up in a few minutes.

"So what brings you to Preston Springs? You said that you were between jobs," Gannon said.

"I was in PR," she said. She didn't like lying to him. "Long story short, I got canned. So I'm working at the family diner until I can land another job."

"I was fired from a job once. I was sixteen and bagging groceries for the local supermarket."

She was grateful he wasn't grilling her about why she'd been fired. "So what happened?"

A dimple creased his cheek when he smiled. "A customer asked me to go in the back and search the hundred plus cartons of milk in stock for the freshest. My brother had just died and my temper was short."

She remembered how terse he'd been on the news reports and what little patience he'd had for public demands for information. "I'm sorry about your brother. What happened?"

"He was a fireman. Died in a house fire when the second floor collapsed on him. The guy who owned the house decided to torch it when his wife won it in the divorce settlement."

A heavy silence settled between them. "I'm very sorry."

"It was a long time ago." But the spark in his eyes had dulled.

Gannon didn't know how the conversation had turned so dark. He'd not talked about Rafe in years. And the last thing he wanted to do was dig up the past. He wanted to be in this moment and only with Darcy.

For some reason talking to Darcy was easy. She had a dry wit and though she'd taken some kind of hit up in D.C., she didn't seem to be wallowing in self-pity.

He still believed she had an agenda, but for now

he wasn't going to worry about it. It was good to be in the company of a woman. He'd spent too much time alone this last year. His mother would be so relieved he wasn't turning into a hermit. She still called him weekly and asked if he'd made any friends.

"What's so funny?" Darcy asked.

He hadn't realized he was grinning. "I was thinking about my mother."

She raised her glass to her lips. "Is this a Freudian thing?"

He laughed out loud. It had been so long since he'd laughed. It felt good, damn good. "No. I promise you it's nothing like that. My mother called last week. She was reading me the riot act about spending too much time alone."

"Glad to hear I could help relieve Mom's worries."

"Believe me, when she calls—and she will call—I'll be sure to report our date. The woman will rest easy."

"If you need me to write a note to prove we had a date, just let me know."

He traced the rim of his glass with his finger. "Will do."

Their meals arrived. She'd ordered the salad, he the hotdog and fries.

"So where is Mom?" she asked popping a cucumber into her mouth.

"Montana."

"Wow, that's a good ways away. I thought you were from D.C."

"The last fifteen years was in D.C. I grew up near Bozeman."

"So how does a Montana boy end up in D.C.?"

"The job."

"And that job would have been…?"

He hesitated. Once someone got wind that he'd worked on the Nero case, they were full of questions he was no longer interested in answering. Especially right now, when it felt like the past was repeating itself. "Worked for the city. Routine stuff."

Her brows lifted with curiosity and he sensed there were more questions rattling around in that pretty head of hers. But she had sense enough to know when not to push. Another point in her column. If he wasn't careful, he could fall for someone like Darcy Sampson.

They spent the next hour talking about the town, laughing about some of the local customs and generally avoiding each other's pasts. Despite her protests, he picked up the check.

When Gannon dropped Darcy off at the Varsity, he was genuinely sorry to see their date end. He'd had a surprisingly pleasant afternoon. For the first time in a long time, he'd forgotten about Nero. He thought back to his meeting with the chief this morning. Maybe he had been looking for trouble where there wasn't any.

She slid her long leg over the side of the bike and hooked her helmet to the seat. "I've got to say this is one fine bike you've got here, Gannon."

He kept his hand on the accelerator so he wouldn't be tempted to touch her. He felt sixteen—awkward and tongue-tied. "Want to go for a ride tomorrow? We could head up into the Shenandoah Valley."

She pushed her tousle of black curls off her face, unmindful of the effect she was having on him. He imagined those curls spread over the pillows on his bed as he made love to her.

She slid her long fingers into her jeans pockets. "Another ride sounds great. I just have to be back by two so I can help prep for the dinner crowd. We had another good sized crowd last night, and it takes all hands on deck to keep up."

Gannon wanted to touch her, see if her skin was as soft as it looked. "No problem. How does ten o'clock sound?"

When she nodded, her curls brushed her high cheekbones. "Great."

On impulse, he reached up and pushed the curl from her face. Silk. "I'll pick you up then."

She moistened her lips. She looked nervous but didn't back away. "Great."

He sensed he would be making love to her soon. "Have a good afternoon."

"You, too." Her voice sounded rusty. "If you get hungry tonight, come by for dinner. I have an in with the owner and can get you a seat no matter how busy it is."

Food was the last thing on his mind right now. "Thanks."

Gannon watched her walk into the tavern, enjoying the way her snug jeans hugged her fanny. He was already wishing away today as he started the bike up again and drove into his shop. When he parked the bike in the garage and shut off the motor, he realized he was whistling.

He'd forgotten what feeling *good* felt like. And he couldn't remember the last time that he'd looked forward to tomorrow.

Casually, he sauntered over to the mailbox outside his shop and grabbed the handful of letters.

An image of Darcy wiping ranch dressing from her lip flashed in his brain. He laughed as he absently started to flip through the envelopes.

When he spotted the plain white envelope, he froze. It didn't have a return address, but it had a Preston Springs postmark.

"Damn."

He opened the envelope.

Inside was a pack of Rome matches.

He flipped open the top of the book. Inside the flap was the message. *The game has begun again.*

Chapter 7

Darcy's good mood vanished when she walked into the bar and saw the dirty floor. She marched directly into the kitchen, past George who was working at the stove, to Trevor's office. She was anxious to give him an earful. He wasn't there.

"George, where is Trevor?"

The black man didn't look up from his pot of stew. "Do I look like a nursemaid?"

"No, do I?"

He studied her a moment. "Yep."

"Well, I'm not." Frustrated, she went into the dining room and called out to her mother. "Mom!"

"What is it, Darcy?" Mrs. Sampson asked,

coming down the back staircase. Her mother looked like she'd had one of her headaches again.

"Where is Trevor?"

"He'll be here," she said wearily.

She checked her watch. Two-ten. "Wasn't he supposed to be here by now?"

Her mother moved into the dining room and behind the bar. She picked up an already clean glass and started to clean it with a cloth. "He's running late."

Darcy dug her fingers through her hair. Showing up on time was common sense. It amazed her they were even having this conversation. "He's not much of a restaurant manager."

Mrs. Sampson set the glass tumbler down hard on the bar. "He does just fine."

"No, he doesn't." Before her mother could argue, she held up her hand. "I'm not arguing with you, Mom. This issue is between Trevor and me. Does he still live on Fifth Street?

"Yes, why?"

Darcy snatched up her keys and her purse which she'd left under the bar. "I'm going to his apartment."

Her mother sighed. "Leave the boy alone. He'll be here soon enough."

"I'm not holding my breath." She started toward the front door.

"You were always jealous of him," Mrs. Sampson said.

Darcy stopped. A surge of anger rolled through her. "Why should I be, Mom?" Sarcasm dripped from each word. "*Maybe* because I became invisible the day he was born. *Maybe* because his sports pictures and trophies decorate the walls of the Varsity and, who knows where mine are. *Maybe* because you never cut me any slack, but you've always made excuses for him."

Mrs. Sampson raised her chin. "You never needed me. You were always strong. Trevor is not strong."

A sad grin tipped the edge of Darcy's mouth. "Oh, I needed you, Mom. I needed you."

Sadness deepened the wrinkles around her mother's eyes. "I can't do this right now."

Guilt stabbed Darcy. "Look, this isn't about who you and Dad loved more. It's business. I need my money or I'm screwed."

"Trevor will get you your money."

"You're damn right he will. And he's going to do it now." She started toward the door.

"You can't leave me. If you're both gone, I can't run this place with just George."

She heard the panic in her mother's voice. "Don't worry, I'll be back within a half hour."

Darcy left the bar and got in her black Corolla. She turned on the ignition. She had less than a quarter of a tank of gas left. Damn. Her life was on vapors.

She put the car in gear and headed over to Trevor's. It took her less than ten minutes to get to the tall, nondescript wooden Victorian house that had long ago been converted into apartments. She took the stairs down to Trevor's basement apartment. She knocked on the door.

No answer.

Darcy pounded on the door. "Trevor!" she shouted. She checked her watch. "It's two-thirty in the afternoon. Open up."

Seconds passed before she heard the shuffle of feet and the scrape of the chain on the door. Trevor cracked the door and looked out. His eyes were bloodshot. "Dee, what are you doing here?"

He smelled of beer and cigarettes. "I need my money, Trevor."

Sleep clung to the corners of his eyes. "I said I'd get it for you."

"You said you'd pay me yesterday. I need my money now." She peered past him into his darkened apartment filled with cigarette smoke. In the small galley kitchen to his right she saw at least twenty empty pizza boxes piled high.

She didn't like having this conversation in the hallway. "Can I come in?"

"The place is a wreck."

Pushing past him, she stepped into the small apartment. The place *was* a wreck. Dirty clothes, bags of garbage and stacks of newspapers littered the floor. The coffee table in front of the black futon couch had three ashtrays on it. All were overflowing with butts.

This went beyond sloppy. "What's going on here, Trevor?"

He pushed a shaking hand through his hair. "What? It's just a little messy."

She faced him. Even in the dim light she could see the dark circles under his eyes. A sick feeling settled in the pit of her stomach. Trevor, like her father, was an alcoholic. And her mother knew it. She was making excuses for Trevor just as she had for their father.

Overwhelming sadness seeped through her body. She'd lived with an alcoholic most of her life, and there'd been times when she didn't think she'd get out with her sanity. But she had gotten out, and until her return home, had thrived.

She knew enough about the disease to know that no amount of talking or pleading would make him stop. The desire to quit drinking had to come from him. "Just give me my money, Trevor."

He shoved a shaking hand through his hair. "I don't think I have my checkbook here."

"Then let's drive over to the tavern and get it now. I'm not kidding. That check I wrote to cover your ass wiped me out. I'm broke."

He rubbed the dark stubble on his chin. "Hey, I'm sorry about that. I'll get your money."

She grabbed his arm. "Let's go."

Trevor jerked his arm away. "I can't go out. I've got to shower first."

Excuses. Her father had been full of them. "I don't care if you look like a bum. We're going now."

He shook his head. "I can't. I've got a UPS delivery coming."

"Leave a note. The rental office can get it."

"No."

"Why not?" His face looked stricken and in that moment she knew. "You don't have the money, do you?"

"I can get it." He sounded like he meant it.

She pressed her fingertips to her temple. "But you don't have it now."

"In a couple of days, I'll have it. I won't stiff you, Dee."

"Man, you sound just like Dad. He always had an excuse for everything."

Trevor's eyes hardened. "I'm not like Dad."

"You are just like him. You are an alcoholic."

"How the hell would you know?"

"I grew up with it."

"Grew up with it," he mocked. "Hell, you

haven't been around for six years. You came home for Dad's funeral and left right after the service. *I* was the one that was here during Dad's illness. *I* was the one that took Mom to the hospital every day. *I* stayed behind and kept the Varsity running so Mom wouldn't be left alone."

"That's not fair." Guilt ate through Darcy's anger, like the cancer that had killed their father. She had ditched her family. But it had been about her survival. She took a step back.

"Yeah, I owe you money, but I'll pay back every stinking dime. You ditched this family when we could have used your help. So you can suck up waiting for your money for a couple of days."

Guilt welled inside her, choking her throat. She almost apologized.

Almost.

Darcy caught herself. Her father and mother had been masters of using guilt to control her. They could squash her anger with a single glance.

"That's good, Trevor, that's real good."

His eyes narrowed. "What is that supposed to mean?"

She saw the empty whiskey bottle by the stove.

"You are more like our old man than I ever thought. Guilt and booze. A lethal combination."

His gaze flickered to the bottle then back to her. The bravado dimmed.

"There is no money, is there?" He started to argue, but she held up her hand to silence him. "No more lies or excuses, Trevor. I just dumped my last penny into the Varsity, and I'm never going to see it again."

"Yes, you will."

Without responding, she turned and stepped into the hallway. The fresh air smelled sweet and she couldn't wait to get out of there.

"Dee," Trevor said. His voice was little more than a whisper. "I will get the money."

"Sure."

Woodenly, Darcy crossed the hall and started up the stairs.

"Dee. Darcy," Trevor said.

She glanced back at him. His shoulders slumped, and he looked a decade older than his twenty-five years. "No more lies, Trevor." She climbed the stairs to the ground floor.

Darcy leaned against the wall by the front door

and closed her eyes. For a moment she was over-whelmed by the mess her life had become.

"Life is not going to beat you," she whispered. "It is not."

She drew in a deep breath. The Nero story was critical to her. Gannon knew more than he was saying. He was the key.

Darcy hated lying to Gannon. She really liked him. But now, more than ever, she needed his help.

With little choice, Darcy returned to the diner and started to prep for dinner.

Trevor showed up at work at six o'clock—early by his standards. To Darcy's great surprise, he was clean-shaven and ready to work. He seemed like his old self.

Neither mentioned the money because the tavern quickly started to fill with customers. Trevor worked the bar, handling his customers with his usual grace. And as the hours wore on, Darcy started to feel that maybe, just maybe, it wasn't as bad as she thought.

The Sampsons fell into a groove very quickly.

Her mother worked the cash register and Trevor stood behind the bar while Darcy waited tables.

At a quarter past seven, Nathan and Larry came into the tavern. Both were in good spirits laughing at a shared joke.

They arrived in time to grab the last booth. Nathan grinned as she handed him his menu. "How are you doing today?"

"Just great," she said grinning.

"You're looking prettier than ever," Larry said as he pulled out a cigarette.

"Thanks, darling," she said. "Heineken and coffee?" she said to Larry and Nathan.

Nathan smiled. "Good memory."

"Glad to see I haven't lost my touch," she said, pleased.

A cigarette dangling from his lips, Larry patted his pockets as he searched for a match. "Hey, you got a match, Darcy?"

"No, but I bet we got some at the bar. Let me get them for you."

Nathan dug a book of matches from his jacket pocket. "Here."

"Thanks," Larry said. "I'm always out of matches.

No matter how many I buy." He opened the pack and lit one and held it to the tip of the cigarette. Puffing, he handed back the matches.

"Keep it," Nathan said. "I've got plenty."

Larry pocketed the matches as Darcy turned toward the bar. She gave Trevor the drink order and filled a bowl of pretzels. She loaded the drinks and pretzels on the tray and headed back to Larry and Nathan's table. "So how go the condos?" she said easily.

"Great," Nathan said as he sipped his coffee. "We are ahead of schedule."

She'd no sooner set the drinks down than the front door opened and Gannon walked in. For a minute, Darcy's mind went blank.

Sexual desire sizzled through her as she watched him stride into the room. He walked with the grace of a lion, each move deliberate and full of power. For reasons she couldn't name, her throat felt dry as she moved toward him.

When did she develop a thing for dangerous men?

Gannon's lips curled into a smile when he saw her. "Working hard?"

"Hardly working," she said in a voice that had thickened.

His gaze didn't leave her. "Looks like you've got a crowd tonight."

She scanned the room for an empty seat. There was none. "I can seat you at the bar in a couple of minutes."

"Don't worry about it. I'll crash their party." Gannon glanced over at the table where Nathan and Larry sat. He walked over to the table. "There room for me?"

Larry ground his cigarette out in the ashtray. "You never come in here."

"Tonight, I am," Gannon said as he shook hands with Nathan. "Mixing up the routine."

"Glad you did," Nathan said.

Larry scooted over to make room for him. "We could use some new blood tonight."

"What can I get you to drink?" Darcy asked.

"Ice water with lemon."

She would have liked to linger but table number six wanted another draft beer and number four wanted ketchup.

She hurried over to the bar where Trevor was mixing a Tom Collins. "Draft. And ice water with lemon."

"Coming right up," Trevor said.

She refilled the peanut bowl for Gannon's table, collected the draft and water, and grabbed a fresh bottle of ketchup. She crossed the room, making her stops at tables four and six.

When she set the water down in front of Gannon, she could see immediately that the tone of the conversation had shifted to serious.

"That fire was no accident," Gannon said. "And the two fires are linked."

Darcy's jaw nearly dropped open. She slowed her pace, hoping to catch a few more snippets of information before she reached the table.

"Well, who would set fires like that?" Larry asked. He'd pulled out another cigarette, but then as if remembering that Gannon didn't smoke, put it away.

"I don't know," Gannon said.

Darcy's gaze was drawn to Gannon's hands. Hands she'd imagined on her body could have set fires that had killed people. The sobering thought sent a chill down her spine.

Managing a smile, she said, "You fellows ready to order dinner?"

★ ★ ★

Gannon liked Darcy's perfume. It was like her. Spicy, unpredictable and sensual. He'd noticed it before she'd reached the table. He'd also noticed that she'd hesitated. She'd been listening to their conversation about the fire.

Why would she care so much about the fires?

He watched her moving around the room from table to table. She wore well-worn hiking boots, jeans and a T-shirt. But the legs. Long, lean and very feminine. Shifting his gaze higher, he lingered on her gently rounded hips and then traveled up the red T-shirt that covered nice round firm breasts.

She moved like a pro. Smiling at the customers, careful to use their names if she knew them, calling them *honey* when she didn't. But he could tell she didn't belong here. She might have grown up working in the tavern, but he guessed she'd not done this kind of work in a long time.

She'd said public relations. It seemed a natural fit, but there was more to the story.

He deliberately avoided talking about the fires again until he noticed that Darcy was within earshot. He'd give her some information but there'd be a payback later. He wanted to know what the hell she was up to.

"I spoke to the chief yesterday about the fires," Gannon said as Darcy approached.

If he hadn't been watching, he'd have missed her slight hesitation.

She set their orders down. "Here you go, boys."

"And?" Nathan said.

"He thinks they're unrelated," Gannon said.

"But you don't," Darcy said.

He half expected her to pull up a stool and sit down. "I only have a gut feeling to go on."

"He's the man that should know," Nathan said. "He investigated fires in his former life."

Darcy didn't seem surprised by the bit of information. But then if she'd been living in D.C., she'd have read about him in the papers. So why not bring it up at lunch?

"Former life is the operative word," Gannon said pulling the tomato off his burger. "Let's not ruin this good meal with talk about fires."

As their chatter settled onto more mundane topics, Darcy drifted away. Over the next hour Gannon lingered, enjoying a hot meal, the company and watching Darcy from the corner of his eye.

He noticed her at the bar with the bartender. He learned from Larry the bartender was her brother. The guy didn't possess her intensity. Relaxed and easygoing, he smiled too much for Gannon's taste.

Darcy's brother was also a heavy drinker. He was careful to drink from a mug, but when Darcy wasn't looking, he filled the cup with coffee and then topped it off with whiskey. At the rate he was going, he'd be hammered by closing time.

At eight-thirty, he said his goodbyes to Larry and Nathan and waved to Darcy who was across the room taking an order.

She'd said earlier she got off at midnight.

Restless, he knew sleep wouldn't come for many hours—if at all tonight. He'd wait until Darcy got off her shift.

And then they'd have a chat about what she was really up to.

Chapter 8

When Darcy dumped the two trash bags into the Dumpster, it was nearly midnight. The customers had cleared out of the tavern and she was cleaning up for the night. Her feet felt as if they'd grown seven sizes over the last few hours. Her body ached.

Not only was she tired but also frustrated. She'd been so busy tonight, there'd been no time to linger near Gannon's table and listen to see if the discussion turned to the fires.

Tomorrow, they had a bike ride planned. She could certainly question him then. But the fact that her professional and personal lines were blurring bothered her. She'd never dated anyone just to get information.

The back door of the tavern banged closed as Trevor came out carrying another bag of trash. He swerved and swayed, and she realized he was drunk.

Without a word to her, he tossed the bag into the Dumpster. He tipped out of balance and would have fallen if she'd not steadied him.

"Man, you are drunk," she said in a voice filled with disgust. "I was stupid to think you were just drinking coffee."

"Where the hell is the money from the register, Darcy?"

"I cleaned out the register a half hour ago and locked the money in the trunk of my car." She'd done this when he'd gone to the men's room. "Tomorrow, I'll deposit it in the bank."

His expression turned savage so quickly it took her breath away. "You did what? That's my money!"

The booze had drowned the natural charmer. "You want me to repeat it?"

"I need that money to pay bills."

"Don't worry, that's exactly what it's going to be used for."

He grabbed her arm. His fingers bit into her arm. "Give me my damn money."

"Why? So you can go buy more booze or maybe you're also into drugs now?"

Trevor wrenched her arm and she let out a painful moan. "Don't play games with me."

"This is no game, Trevor." Like it or not, she couldn't walk away from her brother's problems. She tried to jerk free but couldn't.

"Let go of her." Gannon's deep voice echoed out from the street.

She glanced over Trevor's shoulder as Gannon stepped out of the darkness into the light. He had a brawler's stance, his fists clenched at his sides.

"Butt out!" Trevor shouted.

In three quick strides Gannon crossed the alley and hauled Trevor back with such force he released Darcy and nearly toppled over.

Darcy rubbed the red marks on her wrist. "Go home, Trevor, and sober up."

Trevor straightened his shoulders. He glanced at

Gannon. Even as drunk as he was, he had enough sense to know this was a fight he could not win.

"This isn't over, Darcy," Trevor said.

She watched him stumble down the alley and turn onto the street. "You're right, Trevor, it's far from over," she said more to herself.

Gannon took her wrist in his hand, inspecting the red marks in the streetlight. "Are you all right?"

She pulled away. She didn't deserve his kindness right now. "I'm fine. I'm sorry about my brother."

"He's an alcoholic."

"I know. We already had one knock-down, drag-out earlier today." She pinched the bridge of her nose. "I thought he was doing better tonight. I hoped I'd been wrong."

"He was putting whiskey in his coffee."

She nodded. "Naive to think one good conversation would solve his problem just like that."

"It's not wrong to be hopeful."

"But I was stupid. I should know better." She caught herself. "Look, I'm sorry. You don't need to know the Sampson family problems."

His stance was casual—his hand in his pocket.

However, there was an energy about him that was anything but easygoing.

Tread carefully, she warned herself. "I'd invite you in but Mom is cleaning up."

He pulled his hand out of his pocket and took hers in his. The touch was casual enough but it sent rockets of energy shooting up her arm. "I can make us a pot of coffee at my place."

Alone in his room. Not a good idea. "Thanks. I'll take a pass on the coffee. I'll never sleep if I drink coffee this late."

"I've got decaf." He drew circles on her palm with his fingertip.

If she leaned just a fraction closer, she could kiss him. Taste him. What was wrong with her? "Another time."

"You can ask me about the fires."

She snatched her hand away. "What are you talking about?"

"I knew you were eavesdropping tonight." His voice had an edge to it now.

She could feel the color drain from her face. "It's a hazard of the job. I hear a lot of conversations I'm not supposed to."

The streetlight cast shadows on his face, making him look all the more menacing. "Do you often join in?"

How had he figured her out? "Well, no."

"Let's cut the crap, Darcy. Why do you care about the fires?"

Major backpedaling was in order, but she feared it wasn't going to be good enough. "Everyone in town cares about them."

He stood only inches from her. "There's something more here, Darcy."

Best-case scenario Gannon was going to shut her down when she told him she was a reporter. Worst-case scenario, Gannon was Nero and she'd be admitting to a psycho that she was on to him.

She clenched and unclenched her fingers. "How about we go inside the tavern?"

He didn't budge. "How about you spill it?"

Now or never. And Pulitzers didn't come without sacrifice. "I am a reporter."

"A reporter." He leaned so close she could feel his breath on her face. "Why are you here? Doing a follow-up on a has-been arson investigator? Or a new angle on Nero?"

"A new angle on Nero."

He tightened his jaw. Anger radiated from him. If he was crazy, this could be it for her.

She glanced toward the back door. If she ran, could he catch her before she got inside? Probably. "I need to talk to you about Nero."

For a moment he didn't say anything. He simply stared at her. Headlines flashed in her head: Post Reporter Missing.

Finally, he shook his head, his disgust evident. "You know what? I don't have time for games. Stay the hell away from me, Darcy. We're done." He started to walk away.

Shocked, she stood there a moment. A psycho arsonist wouldn't just walk away, would he? He'd want to know more about why she was here. However, a tired former investigator wouldn't care.

Damn. She didn't know what to think about him now. But either way, if he got away, she'd never have another chance.

She ran in front of him and blocked his path just as he reached the sidewalk. The streetlight above them glowed, giving her some courage. "I'm on a special assignment."

He didn't stop walking. "I don't care."

She hurried to match his pace. "I got a call from a woman about two weeks ago. Sara Highland. Her brother was Raymond Mason—the man everyone said was Nero."

Gannon stopped. "You've got my attention."

"Sara doesn't believe her brother was Nero." She held her breath, ready to run or scream bloody murder if he did anything that seemed remotely dangerous.

He muttered an oath, but didn't leave or approach her.

"At first I figured she was just grieving for her brother and wanted someone to talk to. But the more she talked, the more I started to think she was right. She's been investigating the case on her own. She gave me the name of a man who also believed Raymond wasn't Nero." She sucked in a fresh breath. "The man is homeless and no one seemed much interested in him. I had nothing to lose so I interviewed him. This man believes Raymond was murdered."

Gannon tightened his jaw.

She swiped away a stray curl from her face. "I

agree with Sara. The real Nero lured Raymond to the warehouse so he could fake his own death. And the real Nero didn't die in that last fire in D.C."

It took a moment for her words to sink in. It felt good to know he wasn't the only one who believed Nero was alive. "So you came looking for me?"

"No one knew Nero better than you."

He stared at her a long moment before he said, "Go find another case to solve, Nancy Drew. I don't work with reporters." He started to walk away.

"But if Nero is alive, people are going to die," she said loudly. "Two fires in the last week. Something isn't right."

He kept walking. "Let's face it, you are in this for the headlines, not to save lives."

"Does it matter why I'm in this? What matters is that Nero is stopped."

"I don't trust reporters."

Trust. He could still be an arsonist and he was talking about trust. "Look, it wouldn't be a big deal for you to take time and share your theories with me. I'm not asking for a long-term commitment here."

His gaze sharpened. "I have no theories."

She refused to let him off that easy. "I saw you at that fire this morning. It was weird watching you. It was almost like the fire was talking to you."

He stared at her an extra beat. "I'm not going to help you." He started to walk away.

"We'd make a great team," she shouted.

Gannon didn't even bother to turn around. "I don't like being used."

Gannon was so pissed by the time he got home that he slammed his keys on the desk by the front door of his apartment. To think he'd actually liked Darcy. That he'd had the sense that there was more between them. Something he'd not felt in a very long time.

And she was a damn reporter using him.

He went to the kitchen. He poured fresh water into his coffeemaker and dumped fresh grinds into the filter. The machine started to hiss and spit. Coffee seeped into the pot.

Gannon walked over to his desk by the window and turned on his computer. Darcy was right. When he'd been at the fire today, he had been communicating with it. Fires had their own signature. And if you paid close attention, they could tell you so much.

The fire had been no accident. The blue flames had indicated tremendous heat. A fast-acting accelerant. It had started in the basement—one of the deadliest kinds of fires and a Nero trademark.

When the computer came on, he started to search the Net for recent fires. There weren't many. Brush fires in the Pacific Northwest. Warehouses in New York. But nothing that indicated Nero.

Frustrated, he rose and poured himself a cup of coffee before returning to the computer. The chances of him getting any sleep were slim to none and he'd never be able to concentrate on the bike tonight.

Nero was all he could think about.

He dug the red Rome matches out of his pocket. He flipped them open.

The game has begun again.

Nero was out here.

He could feel it.

Somewhere that bastard was waiting and watching, planning his next fire. Darcy was right about one thing. If he didn't catch Nero, people were going to die.

Darcy believed Nero was alive.

She was the first to speak his deepest fears out loud. For the first time in almost a year, he felt vindicated.

Likely they were the only two people who did believe Nero was alive. And believing didn't mean proving.

Darcy was his only ally.

Gannon slammed the matches on the table. But he'd be damned if he'd work with a reporter. He didn't need her.

He spent most of the night searching the Internet. When that didn't produce anything, he went to his old case files. Slowly, he went over every detail, studying the crime scene photos, the lab reports and the pictures of Nero's victims.

Now he knew he'd been wrong.

The profilers had said Nero had ego. He was intelligent and he liked to game with opponents who would give him a run for his money.

The game has begun again. Nero hadn't set fires this last year because it hadn't been fun. He'd obliterated his identity. Though he was safe, there was no fun anymore.

And now Nero wanted back in the game.

Gannon checked his watch. Eight-fifteen. He picked up the phone and dialed his former boss in D.C. When the secretary answered and he gave his name, she put him right through.

"Well, talk about a voice from the past," Chief Jackson McCray said. The Nero case had been a big boost to McCray's career.

Gannon cradled the phone under his chin. "It's been a long time."

"Too long. It's damn good to hear your voice."

"Same here."

"So how goes it down there in the sticks?"

Preston Springs was hardly the sticks but to Washingtonians anything outside of the metro area was no-man's-land. "It's going well."

"You ever open that garage?"

Small talk had never suited him but he knew he needed to break the ice. "Sure did. In fact, I have a sweet ride that I'll be showing at the Sturgis, South Dakota bike show in August."

"Man, what I wouldn't give to get away from

this desk and get back on a bike." Bikes had been a passion for them both for years. It was one of the few things they'd had in common off the job.

"Come down sometime and I'll lend you a bike. We can ride through the Blue Ridge Mountains."

"I'd love to. But they got me chained to this desk up here." He sighed. "So what can I do for you?"

Gannon knew he'd have to play this just right. "We've had a couple of fires down here."

"Are you helping out the local guys?" His tone wasn't overly serious.

"Tried to, but I think I pissed them off."

Jackson laughed. "Same old Gannon."

He swallowed a surge of resentment. "I think we've got a serial arsonist on our hands." He wished he could ease into the next bit of news, but there was no easy way to say it. "His fires are a lot like Nero's."

"Well, we know it's not that bastard. Some copycat most likely. The press reported most of the details in the paper."

Gannon remembered how he'd argued with McCray last year. That couldn't be Nero. Nero was too smart. But the evidence had continued to support the fact that Nero was dead. And Gannon was so damn tired. So in the end, he'd let himself believe.

Gannon hesitated. "That's the thing. I think Nero is alive."

McCray laughed. "You are crazy, my friend. Nero was bagged and tagged a year ago."

"I'm not so sure."

His tone turned serious. "Gannon, we had forensics work that body—or what was left of it—over from head to toe. The guy left his bag near the scene and it was filled with Nero newspaper clippings."

"They weren't original articles. They were copies."

It was a detail that had always bothered him. "I think Nero copied the articles and planted them."

"What are you smoking? Nero is dead, end of story." He sounded angry.

"I'd still like to follow up. I'd like some help with these fires."

"Look, I know things might get a little dull down in Hooterville. You might be missing the old action. The adrenaline rush. Then along come a couple of fires and you see Nero."

Gannon clenched the phone with his hand so tightly his knuckles turned white. "Believe me, McCray, I don't need this in my life again. No one more than me wanted to see Nero dead. But my gut is telling me he's not."

"Look buddy, I'd like to help you." McCray wanted off the phone. "But I got to get back to work. I'm up to my ass in alligators here."

"I just need the use of your computers for a couple of days. I can be up there by one."

"No way, man. No way. If anyone here got even a whiff that you thought Nero was alive, it would hit the fan. No. Nero is dead and that's final. Hey, my other line is blinking. I've got to go. Good talking to you." He hung up.

Gannon slammed down the phone. Solving the Nero case had boosted McCray's career. And he knew if Nero was found to be alive, his reputation would be tarnished.

Gannon was the only one who believed Nero was alive.

Except Darcy.

She believed.

And she was a reporter with her own agenda. She'd already proved she was a user.

He moved to the window. Darcy passed in front of the tavern window. Her black curls were swept up in a ponytail: she was dressed in a white jog tank, blue shorts and running shoes.

Immediately, his body hardened. She was no good for him. Yet there were parts of his anatomy that had the intelligence of a tree stump. Always would.

Like it or not, Darcy was his only ally.

This time around he'd be the one using the press, not the other way around.

Chapter 9

Darcy was a half mile into her run when she heard the roar of the motorcycle engine. Gannon. Darcy didn't need to look behind her to know it was him. She kept running. If he wanted to talk to her, he was going to have to work for it.

She picked up her pace. The engine grew louder and she wished she'd brought her iPod so she could drown out the sounds with music.

Suddenly, she saw the flash of metal as Gannon's motorcycle skidded to a stop in front of her, blocking her path.

Wiping the sweat from her eyes, she stopped.

Her heart hammered in her chest. "What do you want?"

He flipped up his visor. "Get on."

"Why?" The idea of a lecture didn't appeal to her right now.

His tone was angry, frustrated. "You want to find Nero or not?"

That had her attention. "Why the change of heart?"

"You've got contacts that can help?"

She suspected this alliance cost him. "Yes."

His jaw tensed and released. "I can't catch him alone. I'm going to need your help."

Darcy wanted to shout a whoop at her good fortune. The pessimist in her had her asking, "Again, why the change?"

He muttered an oath. "Get on or work alone. I'm not having this conversation with you in public when anyone could be watching."

Tension in his voice slashed through her bravado. She tried not to glance around. "Do you think Nero could be watching?"

Gannon flipped down his visor and revved his engine as if he were going to leave.

"All right!" She hurried toward the bike and un-hooked the helmet from the back seat. "I'm kinda sweaty."

"I've smelled worse." He waited while she put on the helmet, climbed on the back and grabbed ahold of his waist. He could feel his racing heartbeat in his chest under her arms.

He checked for traffic and pulled out onto the street. Though the sun was warm, the wind blast-ing against her sweaty body left her freezing.

They drove through town south on Route 29. He weaved in and out of traffic easily, as if he and the bike were one. Darcy was amazed how quickly her body relaxed against his.

When they reached an elementary school in the center of town, he pulled over to the side. Reluc-tantly, she released him, already missing his heat. But she wasn't about to start complaining.

Gannon climbed off and pulled off his helmet. He took Darcy's from her and hooked them to the bike. "There's a table over here where we can sit."

They sat at a small picnic table under the shade of an oak tree. Though the day was warm, she felt chilled to the bone. Gannon shrugged off his jacket and handed it to her.

"Thanks, I'm fine. Besides I'm sweaty."

"Put the jacket on."

Grateful for the warmth, she shrugged it on. The jacket smelled of Gannon. Masculine. She almost felt as if his arms were wrapped around her. "So why the school?" she asked hoping the knot in her stomach would release.

"First, we strike a deal. I don't want any secrets. You lie to me and I'll cut you off."

"Information is a two-way street. You cut me out and I walk, too."

He stared at her a long moment. "Agreed. I also don't want you going public with anything unless I give the okay. You start leaking information before I say so and I'll cut the flow of information off immediately."

"I don't like having my stories controlled by anyone but me."

The glint in his eyes told her this was non-negotiable. "Decide now, Darcy. That's the condition of my help." He leaned toward her. "What I have to say will put you back on the map."

She had no doubt his information was good. What worried her was his true motive. Did he want to stop Nero or was he Nero?

"Deal," she said. They had shared nothing as formal as a handshake. Each knew where the other stood.

He nodded. "You are right about Raymond Mason. I think he was set up."

Darcy's heart rate accelerated. "Can you prove it?"

"Not yet."

She tamped town her frustration. "Then how do you know he wasn't Nero?"

"My gut. Nero was just too damn smart to make a stupid mistake such as not knowing the back door to the warehouse was bolted. His attention to detail was superb. Add in the fact that I was getting too close to Nero. I think he panicked and pulled out of the game."

"Do you know who he is?"

Frustration deepened his frown. "No. But I feel like I know him. And I know he is close."

Her skin tingled. "Tell me about him."

"He is in his mid-thirties or forties. There's a

certain air of maturity about his letters and messages, yet, his handwriting isn't that of an old man. He loves control."

"Education?"

"I'd say very educated, college, graduate school even. The games, the puzzles, he loves them all." He turned and faced her. She noted the small scar on his chin and was tempted to trace it with her fingertip. She didn't. "He dresses well, very neat. All his fires were very organized, the accelerants lined up in straight rows."

"He loved the attention."

"He is addicted to it."

"What if you left town? Would he stop?"

"For a while. Then he'd follow and the fires would start up again." His gaze held hers. "It's not just about the fires. It's about the hunt."

"It sounds like you crawled in his head."

"I did."

"You keep saying *he*. You are certain Nero is a man."

"Yes."

She wished she had her pad and pencil. "Have you called the arson team in D.C.?"

"Yeah. They won't touch this one because if Nero is alive, then that means they were all wrong a year ago. Too many careers were built after Nero's death."

Disgust ate at her. "So why the school?" she said refocusing.

He stared at the sunny brick building with the brightly colored pictures taped in the class-room windows. "If Nero's pattern holds true, this school—or one like it—will be the next target."

A sick feeling tightened her gut. "There's two weeks of school left. Hundreds of children go to this school."

"The last school he torched went up at lunch-time. The school had a quick-thinking principal and he had his kids out of the school in record time. No one was killed but if he'd delayed even three minutes, the children in the west wing would have been killed when the roof collapsed."

"My God."

"Nero is one sick bastard, Darcy. And I need you to understand that this is more than just a story. It's about stopping someone who is very evil."

A cold chill snaked down her spine. "Have you alerted the chief?"

"I have. He thinks I'm either a nut, a burnout or someone poaching on his territory. I'm going to stop by the police after I drop you off, but I'm not holding out much hope for them either."

"Do you have any proof?"

Gannon reached in his pocket and pulled out the two books of Rome matches. He opened the flaps and showed her the inscription.

She studied the thick bold lettering. "Everyone in D.C. knew about the matches."

"Look at the ink."

"It's green."

"A green fine-tipped marker. That is a detail that never made it to the papers."

"You're basing all this on green ink. That could be a lucky coincidence." Great. Maybe Gannon was a nut. Maybe this was a setup.

He sighed. "There's more to it than ink. It's the shape of the *a*'s. The way he presses down when he writes. It's him. I'd bet my life on it."

She rubbed her fingers over the gold embossed letters of Rome. "We're going to need more evidence than matches and Raymond's sister to prove Nero is alive. D.C. has a lot of hard evidence that proves Raymond was Nero. You tell me what's more credible."

"I've thought a lot about the hard evidence over the last year. All of it could have been staged."

"Why would Nero come back after all this time? It can't just be boredom."

"Nero can't walk away from the fires any more than Trevor can walk away from the booze. Like I said, he's addicted to the rush."

Addiction. Compulsion. Disease. How many times had she heard those terms growing up? "I know what a tight hold the demons can have on a man."

His shoulders relaxed a fraction. "Let's go back to my apartment. My old case files are there."

Darcy hesitated. Gannon fit his own description of Nero. And here she was ready to follow him to his apartment.

When he noticed she wasn't following, he stopped and said, "Are you coming?"

Now or never, Sampson. "Yeah, I'm coming."

★ ★ ★

Two hours later, Darcy sat in the corner of Gannon's apartment with a half-dozen folders spread out around her.

Sunlight streamed through the apartment's tall windows. The apartment was furnished simply with a couch and a large eating table with a couple of chairs around it. There was no TV in sight but stacks of books lined the walls as if expecting Gannon to build bookshelves for them. In the far left corner of the room was his bed, rumpled and twisted sheets testifying to a restless night's sleep. To her right, a galley kitchen with a small stove and refrigerator, which she suspected was empty.

Since she'd arrived, she'd done nothing but read Gannon's case folders as he paced. Finally, when she could take his pacing no more, she told him to sit and be still. He'd sat at his dining table and started to work on designs for another bike. Though he said nothing, she knew his thoughts weren't far from her.

Gannon's notes were meticulous. He had explored every aspect of Nero, including the man's background, possible professions, his reasons for setting the fires, and even a physical description.

According to Gannon's notes, Nero likely had a steady job. Raymond Mason had gotten his degree but had not held a steady job since he'd left the army.

The muscles in her shoulders ached as she picked up an article from last year—one that Barbara Rogers had written.

What interested her was not the article but the picture of Gannon standing at the podium during a statement to the press.

Dressed in a coat and tie, his eyes were dark and angry. Deep lines in his forehead had faded somewhat. He looked so worried and concerned. This wasn't the face of a man who was setting fires. This was the face of a man frustrated that he couldn't stop a killer.

She glanced up at Gannon. He studied the paper in front of him, but he wasn't drawing. Those same lines had returned to his face. He was desperate to catch Nero.

In that moment, she *knew*.

Gannon was not Nero.

Darcy sat back in her chair. Unreasonable relief flooded through her body.

"You look ten years younger now," she said laying another article aside.

He glanced up from the sketch and set his pencil down. Seemingly relieved to have the silence broken, he rose and moved toward her. "I felt two hundred when that picture was taken. Nero was torching the city and my wife had just left me."

He'd been married. She glanced at his naked ring finger. Whatever tan lines his wedding band might have left were completely gone. "I'm sorry."

He flexed the fingers on his left hand. "About the fires or my divorce?"

"Both. The divorce. I've been left. I know how it hurts."

He studied her as if he were trying to read her thoughts. "Looks like you've moved on."

The last thing she wanted to do was talk about Stephen. "And you, too."

A grim smile tipped the edge of his lips. "We're a couple of survivors."

"Yeah." Uncomfortable with the personal line of conversation she said, "I see similarities to the fires here. It's not just the locations. They have the same feel."

He nodded thoughtfully. "Nero has a specific style and burn pattern."

"So what do we do?"

"I'm going to set up cameras in places where I think he'll strike. Then I'm going to start talking about Nero and let it be known I think he's a coward."

"How do you know he'll hear what you're saying about him?"

He didn't look the least bit worried. "He's close. I can feel it."

She kept her voice even, but her nerves jumped. "What do I do?"

"I don't think he has been completely dormant this last year. I think there've been other fires. Smaller, likely not more than one or two in a city, but fires nonetheless. I need for you to start searching databases to see what pops up."

"I'll call my editor at the paper. He'll do a search for me if I give him the guidelines." Then before he could say anything, she said, "He knows I'm down here investigating Nero. And he is expecting to hear from me."

He shoved out a breath as if willing his body to

relax. "All right. Call him. Tell him we are looking for school, restaurant, church and hotel fires. Those are Nero's favorite targets."

Nodding, she pulled her cell phone off her waistband and dialed her editor. The phone rang three times and for a moment she feared Paul wasn't in his office. Finally, he picked up. "Paul Tyler."

"Paul, it's me, Darcy." She could feel Gannon's gaze on her.

"Darcy? It's about time you called. What have you found out so far?" Paul asked.

"I made contact with Gannon." From the corner of her eye, she could see his frown deepen.

"Good. Have you learned anything?"

She quickly explained about the new set of fires in Preston Springs and their similarity to the Nero fires in Washington.

Paul listened without comment but she could almost hear him frowning through the phone. "Darcy, I want you to be careful. Gannon is a suspect as far as I'm concerned."

She lowered her voice. "Let's not get into that right now."

"Is Gannon with you now?"

"Yes." She glanced at Gannon. He leaned against the exposed brick wall, his arms folded over his chest.

Darcy could picture Paul peering over his black half-glasses and staring out his small window that overlooked the street. "I don't want you getting hurt."

"Everything is under control."

"Famous last words."

She ignored that comment. "Paul, I need you to do a search for me. I'm specifically looking for arson fires in the last year—schools, restaurants, churches and hotels. Chances are these fires won't be huge, but they'll match Nero's MO."

Papers rustled in the background. Darcy could imagine Paul shuffling through the mountain of papers on his desk as he searched for a pen. "Consider it done. Anything else?"

"No, that's it for now."

Paul's chair squeaked as she leaned forward. "Has he given you any good information?"

"I've studied his case files. They're very detailed and helpful. And Paul, for now, keep this to yourself."

"No problem. I'll get on this search. I'll call you soon."

Gannon moved beside Darcy. He stared at her, blue eyes penetrating. She felt skittish when he was close—it was hard to breathe evenly.

"Thanks." Darcy put the receiver down. "He's going to do the search in a couple of hours."

"Good."

Gannon walked to the window. He stared out at the clouds drifting by, the azure sky. "There are going to be more fires and soon."

Nervous, she moved to his kitchen where she'd seen a coffeepot earlier. The pot was half full. She poured a cup. It tasted like mud. "Who taught you how to make coffee?"

The light in the window slashed across his face. "I learned from an old fireman. He liked it strong."

She poured the cup down the sink. "Drinking battery acid has more appeal. Where do you keep your coffee grinds?"

"Above the sink. You don't have to do that. I'll make another pot."

"No, no," she said holding up her hand. "Let the

professional handle this. I've been making coffee in the tavern since I was six."

She found the grinds, dumped out the old. Soon, she was brewing a fresh pot.

He sat on the stool on the other side of the counter and stared at her. "So how did you get from here to D.C.?"

"A long story. And Nero is more important."

"We've got a few spare minutes. Spill it, Sampson. Why'd you run away from home?"

His comment struck a nerve. "Not much to tell. Dad was a drinker. Mom was always in denial. Trevor was the golden child. I never fit. For as long as I can remember I wanted out. I earned a scholarship to Hollins University. I got my degree while working in the tavern. The day I graduated I packed up and left." She pulled two fresh cups from the cabinet and set them on the counter. "I'm boring."

"No, you're not." A half smile tugged the edge of his lips, but there was no mirth attached to it. "You're remarkable." She saw raw sexual desire in his eyes.

Uncomfortable, she said. "So why the switch to bikes?"

He didn't question her need to shift the spotlight off her life. "Always loved 'em. My old man used to build them. My brother Rafe and I would sit for hours and watch him work. But my kid sister Darla is the genius when it comes to machines. 'Fact, she's crewing on the NASCAR circuit now as a mechanic."

"Impressive." The coffee finished brewing and she filled both the cups.

"No sugar in the house but there is milk in the refrigerator."

"Great."

She got the milk and poured what few drops were left in the carton into her cup. "What is it with guys? Two drops left in the milk carton and they still stick it back in the fridge?"

He laughed.

Smiling, she handed him his cup. As he reached for it, his fingers brushed hers.

The sexual chemistry between them snapped. The laughter in his eyes vanished. She knew he'd take her right here in the kitchen if she said the word. Her pulse throbbed in the base of her throat. Her mouth felt dry and her stomach tightened.

In that instant, Darcy knew it wasn't a matter *if* they landed in bed, but *when*.

Chapter 10

Gannon's body went hard as he stared at Darcy. He'd been doing his best to ignore the tension between them since she climbed on his bike today and hugged her body close to his. He'd felt her breasts pressing against his back and her bare thighs brushing his hips. Throughout the ride, he kept imagining those long legs of hers wrapped around him as he drove into her.

A sane man would have sent her away and taken a cold shower. Distance. Perspective. That's what he needed.

But he didn't give a damn about distance or perspective right now. He wanted to taste Darcy.

Setting his cup down, he moved around the counter and before either could analyze too much, he took her face in his hands and kissed her on the lips.

The kiss was gentle at first. Strictly exploratory. And he half expected her to belt him and tell him to get lost.

But she didn't.

Her lips parted slightly and she relaxed into him. Needing no more encouragement, he teased her lips open wider with his tongue. She accepted him without hesitation.

Darcy wrapped her long bare arms around him and deepened the kiss. God, but she tasted so good.

Her rapid pulse beat through the sleek fabric of her tank top and tapped against his chest. Her excitement matched his own.

Gannon pressed his erection against her thin jogging pants. She moaned softly.

He allowed his hand to drop to her shoulders and then down her spine to her backside. He squeezed her buttocks gently and pushed her against him. Still kissing her, he guided her toward the bed. When the back of her legs bumped into the edge of the bed, he eased her back toward the soft mattress.

He cupped her breast and through the fabric of her jogging top, teased her nipple into a hard peak. "I want to be inside you."

Darcy froze at the sound of Gannon's voice. Thick with desire and passion, it broke the spell. Reality crashed through the haze of desire. Losing control wasn't her style, especially in the bedroom. And she was on the verge of throwing caution to the wind.

She moved her face from his, breaking the kiss. "No, Gannon."

He was already reaching for his belt buckle when she spoke. His hand stilled. His face was only inches from hers. "What's wrong?" The words sounded torn from his throat.

"This is not smart, Gannon."

He kept his hand on her shoulder, as if she were a skittish mare, not a woman who knew when she was crossing the line. "I know."

She moistened her lips with her tongue. "And as much as I'd like your hands on me, there are practical reasons why we can't do this. And I'm not just talking about condoms."

He dropped his head to the nape of her neck. The stubble on his jaw brushed her bare skin like sandpaper. "Are you married? Engaged?" He didn't sound like he cared for either option.

"No."

Gannon raised his head and looked her in the eyes. "Then why not?"

She scooted out from under him, needing distance. "We are working together."

"I can maintain perspective." He sat up and shoved his long fingers through his hair.

She wasn't sure if that was true. But she knew she couldn't sustain any sort of balance if they started sleeping together. "I don't mix business with sex."

Gannon watched Darcy move to the other side of the counter. Today had been chock-full of surprises. "Fair enough."

"Look, I better go now."

Those long legs of hers would stick with his memory for a good while. He shoved his hand in his pocket. "Right." A cold shower was definitely in order. "I'll start assembling surveillance equipment, place them at high risk areas."

"Great." She stumbled toward the door. Her hair was mussed and her cheeks flushed. He wasn't the only one who needed a cold shower. "I'll call as soon as I hear from Paul."

"Sure."

She half walked, half ran out the door. Moving across the apartment to the window that overlooked the alley separating their buildings, Gannon watched her disappear into the tavern.

"When this mess is over, Darcy, I'll make love to you properly."

Nero sat outside the elementary school, watching the children play on the playground. Several boys swung from monkey bars, others played touch football while the girls gathered near the swings to whisper secrets that made them all laugh. The teachers visited on a park bench while glancing periodically at the playground.

The day was beautiful, the sky a deep azure and the breeze soft and gentle. It was a perfect day for a fire.

He stared at the school's brick exterior, imagining his red flames dancing as they devoured the structure. His fires would sway and bend beautifully in the gentle wind today, moving like an exquisite ballerina's arms swaying in time to the symphony's music.

He checked his watch. Twelve o'clock.

His fire would come alive in one hour—when all the children were back inside for their afternoon classes.

The only fly in the ointment was the timetable. Nero wanted to take more time in between the fires. He didn't like to rush. The time after a fire was like the afterglow of great sex. This was the time he studied the damage his fires wrought, drank in the newspapers' reports and soaked up the talk of people who worried when he'd strike next.

But the game was different this time.

It was faster paced.

More dangerous.

More thrilling.

Given too much time, Gannon would catch him this time. The investigator was smart and had learned from his past mistakes. If he didn't move quickly, Gannon would catch him and lock him up for the rest of his life.

And he had no intention of going to jail.

Nero climbed back into his truck and started the engine. Gannon would be receiving his pack of Rome matches as the fire started. But even if Gannon sprinted across town, he would not reach the school to warn everyone.

Whistling, Nero started the truck and headed back to work.

After Darcy left, Gannon tracked down a guy in town who owned three surveillance cameras and was willing to rent them to him. The problem was that there were nine schools in the city—seven elementary, one middle and a high school. He'd never be able to cover all nine with three cameras.

Spreading out a map of the city he marked each school with a red dot. Nero would most likely go for the school that would garner the most attention. Elementary, most likely. And definitely, in the center of town. He wanted people to watch his fire. And he wanted them afraid.

There were three schools in the immediate area.

They were positioned for the greatest splash. And Nero liked splash.

Bastard.

For a moment Gannon closed his eyes. Damn, but he felt helpless. Rage rolled over him like a wave. The son of a bitch was alive. And he was going to kill again.

He checked his watch. Twelve thirty. There'd been thirty-six hours between the first two fires. In D.C. Nero had set his first three fires fourteen days apart. Then the pattern had dropped to every four days apart and then two. Now, however, it was anybody's guess when Nero would strike again.

Gannon gathered up his papers and headed downstairs to the garage. He was going out the back door when a courier rode up on a bike. The kid was tall, lanky—most likely a college student earning an extra few bucks. He wore a red-and-white cycle racing jersey.

The courier stopped his bike, checked the address of the building. "You Michael Gannon?"

"That's right."

"Got a delivery for you, dude."

Gannon accepted the white envelope. He didn't

need to open it to know it was from Nero. "There's a twenty in it if you can tell me who sent this." He dug the money out of his pocket.

"Don't know. It was given to me by dispatch. Oh, but I do know I was told not to deliver it to you until one o'clock." The kid checked his watch and grinned. "I got a class at one. I was going to drop it off afterwards but this girl I know asked me to help her study. She's a fox and I didn't want to disappoint her."

Gannon handed the kid the twenty.

"Thanks, dude," the kid said.

Gannon didn't acknowledge the kid's thanks or notice him drive off as he ripped open the envelope. Inside was the picture of an elementary school. White columns, tall bushes and a cement sidewalk but no sign and no identifying marks. It would take him time to figure out which school this was—time he didn't have.

Darcy would know. She'd been raised in Preston Springs.

He ran across the street and tried the front door. It was locked. Cursing, he ran down the alley to the back of the restaurant. Opening the kitchen door, he dashed inside. An older woman stood by the stove. She glanced at him, her eyes wide with shock.

"Where's Darcy?" he demanded.

"Who wants to know?" Though her hair had turned to gray, she had the same sharp gaze as Darcy.

"Damn it, where is she? This is an emergency!"

"She's upstairs in the shower," the woman said.

He started toward the back staircase.

"I'm going to call the police," she shouted.

"Fine." He took the stairs two at a time. "Darcy!"

Darcy rounded the corner at the top of the stairs. Her hair was wet and she wore pants and flip-flops. She clutched a blue shirt over her bra. "I heard you screaming. What's wrong? I thought someone had died."

He raced up the stairs and thrust the picture at her. "What school is this?"

Quickly she pulled on her shirt. "It's Morgan Elementary."

"Where is it?"

"Long Street."

"Show me."

He took her by the hand and half pulled her down the stairs. When they reached the kitchen, Mrs. Sampson was standing with a kitchen knife in one hand and the phone in the other. "You let her go!"

Gannon knew where Darcy got her loud voice.

"Its okay, Mom," Darcy said as he towed her through the kitchen. "Mr. Gannon is my friend."

Her eyes narrowed. "You're not being kidnapped?"

"No."

Gannon opened the back door and paused. "Call the fire department and tell them to get to Morgan Elementary school."

"I don't take orders from you!"

"Mom, please," Darcy pleaded. "Just do it."

Her mother was mumbling something about rudeness and this was the last straw as she dialed the fire department.

Darcy struggled to keep up in her flip-flops as they ran into his garage. He pushed the bike outside and started the engine as she hopped on the back. Not bothering with helmets, they skidded out the garage door.

"Is this Nero's next target?" she shouted against his ear.

He barely stopped at a stop sign before he rolled on through toward the school. "Yes."

Five minutes later he stopped his bike by the front door of the school, parking on the front lawn. He checked his watch. Ten minutes to one o'clock. "He's going to set the fire at one o'clock."

"How do you know?" she asked following him up the brick steps.

"It's in his note."

Gannon glanced at the school office sign. "Dammit, I don't have time to argue with people."

Darcy brushed past him and toward the fire alarm on the wall. "Then, don't." She pulled the lever.

A loud buzzer started blaring in the concrete halls and red lights on the wall started to flash. Immediately, students started filing out of their classrooms and heading out the exits.

The principal hurried out the office. His tie was loose, his sleeves rolled up to his elbows. "What is going on here? If that Nick Bernard pulled the alarm again, I'll suspend him for the rest of his life."

"I pulled the fire alarm," Darcy said.

"Is this some kind of joke?"

Gannon stepped between them. "No joke. I think you're going to have a fire today."

"You think."

"Look, I'll explain everything, but I need for you to clear this building."

As the alarm wailed, the principal studied him a moment then hustled back into the office. Seconds later he announced, "Teachers, administrators and staff. Vacate the building immediately. This is not a drill."

The principal followed Gannon and Darcy out of the building. "This better be on the level," he said as he adjusted the frequency of a walkie-talkie he'd picked up in the office.

The parking lots and playgrounds quickly filled with children. In the distance, the fire truck's sirens blared as the engines got closer and closer.

Gannon glanced at his watch. The long hand clicked to one o'clock. For several seconds nothing happened. He was aware of Darcy behind him, her body pressed close to his back.

Children talked and laughed—grateful to be out of class again so soon after lunch. The teachers and administrators nervously glanced at the principal. The fire engines grew closer.

And there was no fire. Seconds ticked by.

The principal walked up to Gannon. "You mind telling me what the devil is going on here?"

"There's going to be a fire in the building."

"You said already. How do you know this?"

"There have been two other fires in town."

"Yeah, so. What does that have to do with my school?"

"I think yours is next." He thrust the paper at the principal. "He said it would burn today at one o'clock."

"Who's he?"

"Nero."

Before the principal could question him further, the engines screeched around the corner. Red lights flashing, the two engines parked in front of the school. The captain climbed down off the engine and strode over to the principal as his men pulled hose lines from the two red engines and unloaded axes and crowbars. "What's going on here?"

"This man says there is going to be a fire in the school any minute."

The captain met Gannon's steady gaze. "You're Gannon, right?"

Great. The chief had warned his men about him. "Yeah, that's me."

The captain shook his head. "Buddy, you are a real nut job, aren't you?"

Gannon didn't care if they called him the village idiot right now. As long as the children were out of the school. He handed the picture to the captain.

"How do I know you didn't take this?" the captain said.

Darcy stepped forward. "He didn't."

He arched a bushy brow. "And you know this why?"

She brushed a wet curl off her face. "He came to me. He needed help finding the school."

He muttered an oath. "So you only have his word."

Challenge sparked in her eyes. "That's right."

"Oh, well, that makes it better." He shook his

head and pulled off his hat, running his fingers through his thick black hair.

The principal shook his head. "Can my kids go back inside the school?"

Gannon would block the damn entrance with his body if need be. "Don't send them in, yet. Give it a few more minutes."

The captain glanced at his watch. "It's five after one. Your fire is late."

Gannon stared at the school. "A few more minutes won't make a bit of difference."

The captain studied him. "I'll send my men in to check the school out."

"Don't," Gannon said. "If this arsonist follows his patterns, there will be a timer on a can of gasoline in the basement rigged to explode."

The captain shook his head. "Principal, how many ways are there into the basement? I want to send my men in."

Before the principal could answer, a loud explosion radiated from the basement, shaking the building and blowing out several of its windows. The children and teachers screamed and drew back. Within seconds the school was engulfed in flames.

The principal glanced at the hundreds of children and then at Gannon. His face turned deathly pale. If the children had been inside the building, they would be fighting for their lives. The principal turned and ran toward the teachers, ordering them to get the children away from the school.

Three shades paler, the captain called the police and reported the explosion as his men scrambled with the hoses. "Don't leave my sight," the captain said to Gannon. "You've got a hell of a lot to explain."

"Whatever you want to know." Gannon stared at the children. He released his first full breath since he'd opened the note.

"My God, look at those flames," Darcy said. "And all those children."

Before Gannon could explain, a Washington, D.C., Channel Five news crew pulled into the school parking lot. Immediately, the crews started filming.

Gannon tensed. The front door of the news van opened and out came Stephen Glass. His blond hair perfect, he wore charcoal suit pants, a blue dress shirt and red tie. Glass walked with the swagger of an athlete.

It had been a year since Gannon had seen the reporter, but he'd still dearly love to punch him out.

"Did you call him?" Gannon demanded.

"No," Darcy said. She looked as shocked as he felt.

Glass shrugged on his suit coat and strode over to Gannon. He flashed the million-dollar smile that won him big points during the rating sweeps.

Darcy turned away from Glass, muttering something about rotten luck and murder. He had only a moment to wonder what her connection to Glass was before the reporter shoved a mike in his face.

"Michael Gannon. Care to comment on Nero's latest fire?"

Struggling with murderous thoughts, Gannon stared at Stephen.

Stephen kept smiling, seemingly enjoying Gannon's rage. "How did you get fire crews here so quickly? Did you have prior knowledge of the fire?"

Gannon said nothing, so Glass shifted his focus

to Darcy. In one easy move, Glass moved passed Gannon and gave Darcy a kiss on the lips. "Miss me, gorgeous?"

Chapter 11

Stephen tasted of cigarette smoke and stale coffee. She jerked away and wiped her mouth with the back of her hand. "What are you doing here?"

"I could ask you the same, Darcy," Stephen said still grinning.

Darcy was very aware of Gannon's gaze on her. "I was here first, Stephen."

"I was in Richmond covering a story when I got a call on my cell from Barbara." Barbara's office was next to Paul's. "Barbara heard Paul on the phone talking to you about Nero."

Darcy swallowed an oath. She could picture the scene. Paul hadn't closed his door and Barbara had listened in on the conversation. It happened all the time in the newsroom. "So she figured she'd give you a call."

He winked. "That's right. And since I was less than an hour away covering another story, I said I'd stop by. We picked up this fire on the police scanner."

Darcy ground her teeth. "This is my story, Stephen."

He grinned. "All's fair in love, war and reporting."

Gannon stepped forward. His gaze bore into Stephen. "Friend, Darcy?"

"We used to be," Darcy said.

The heat of the blaze bore down on them. The teachers had already backed the children up across the road so that they were far from the school. More fire trucks were also arriving.

Stephen grinned liked the Cheshire cat. He knew his arrival had stirred up something and he was enjoying it. "Now, come on babe, it was more than that."

Darcy looked at Gannon. "You and I need to talk."

"You don't owe me an explanation." He turned on his heel and stalked off toward Chief Wheeler who'd just pulled up in his car.

This wasn't the best time to discuss old boyfriends, but Darcy owed Gannon an explanation, and he was going to get one whether he wanted it or not. She started after him. She made it five steps before Stephen came up behind her and grabbed her by the arm.

The bastard was all smiles. "So what's the scoop here, babe?"

"Get lost, Stephen." She saw Gannon disappear into the crowd.

"Is that all you got to say to me?"

"Let go of me." She'd never been angrier. "Or you'll be singing high notes for the rest of your life."

He released her and held up his hands in surrender. "I just figured since we were pals you'd help me out."

"Pals?" She nearly choked on the word. "Most of my *pals* don't screw me and then dump me for the first available blonde."

He winced. "I didn't dump you."

She let her anger bubble to the surface. "Oh, that's right, you said we were taking a break so you could figure out a few things."

"What's wrong with that?"

There'd been a time when she'd thought he was everything she'd been looking for. Sophisticated, funny, charming, he was unlike any man she'd known growing up in Preston Springs. If she'd bothered to look beyond the expensive suits and porcelain teeth, she'd have seen a vain, selfish man. "I'm not going to waste my breath explaining."

He looked the picture of innocence. "She didn't mean anything to me."

Disgust rose in her throat. "You're wasting my time." She started in Gannon's direction.

He did his best hurt puppy dog look as he hurried beside her. "God, Darcy. I loved you."

"Yeah, yeah." That look would have worked on her two years ago. It didn't now.

His eyes hardened when she kept walking. "When did you turn into such a bitch?"

"Ah, there is the real Stephen."

"Okay, so I might have screwed up the thing we had."

She clenched her fingers. "Cut the crap, Stephen. You don't want me, you want an angle on this story."

"Baby, I love you."

She laughed so hard tears pooled in her eyes.

Pursing his lips, he seemed to get that his tactics weren't working. "Is Nero alive or not?" He had to hurry to keep pace with her as she moved around the edge of the crowd. There was no sign of Gannon.

"How should I know?"

"Barbara heard everything Paul said."

"Yeah, well she got it all wrong. I don't know what you are talking about."

"You are a bad liar, Darcy."

Gannon was nowhere in sight. Disappointment chewed at her. She'd blown things with him and the thought left her deeply sad. "Sue me."

His smile lost its boyish charm and turned menacing. "It doesn't really matter if he's alive or not. I really don't care. But just the idea that he might be will get me a hell of a lot of airtime."

Darcy looked at Stephen. In him she saw herself. When she'd arrived in Preston Springs, Nero had been no more than a story. She wasn't as concerned about lives as headlines. No wonder Gannon had been so angry when he found out she was a reporter.

As the sirens blared, school buses arrived to take the children away. She thought about all the children who could have died today.

Nero was more than a headline.

He was a psychopath who needed to be stopped.

"Hell, I bet I could even spin the story to suggest that our Mr. Gannon is Nero. I mean who knew the fires better than him? Maybe he's orchestrated all this so that he can get himself back in the limelight."

Darcy stopped in her tracks. God, she'd had the same theories about Gannon. "Do you know how many children could have died today if he hadn't been here?"

"The more casualties the better the ratings."

Stephen made her physically sick. "You are a real bastard, Stephen."

He shrugged casually. "We've all got our crosses to bear."

Slowly she unclenched her fingers. "Leave Gannon out of this."

Surprise flickered in his eyes before they narrowed. "You got a thing going with the arson investigator?" He touched her shirt, which she realized was inside out. She'd dressed so quickly when Gannon had arrived she'd never bothered to check. "You guys having a little fun this morning?"

She smacked his hand away. "Drop dead."

Darcy thankfully didn't have to walk the two miles back to the Varsity in flip-flops. Gannon had asked one of the policemen to give her a ride, which she'd gratefully accepted.

When she arrived at the tavern, George was in the kitchen standing over a pot of stew. "Your mother and brother aren't here."

A headache pounded in the back of her skull. "Where are they?"

"Trevor is out, like always. And your mother is upstairs with a sick headache. She says you can run the register tonight." Her mother always got sick headaches when things had been especially bad with her father.

An oppressive weight bore down on her chest. She was drowning in her family's problems. "Me? I haven't run the register in ten years."

He shrugged his thick shoulders as he stuffed sage and garlic in a chicken. "I am just the cook."

"Yeah, and I'm just the dumb sap who didn't have the sense to stay away from home."

He grimaced. "So are you going to run the register or not?"

Before she could answer, the sound of a motorcycle engine roared down the alleyway. "George, how about you take the rest of the day off?"

He lifted an eyebrow. "I've already made the salads and the stews."

She had more important things to handle than the cash register. "Will they keep until tomorrow?"

"Sure."

"Then wrap it all up and take the rest of the day off."

He lifted a bushy brow. "I can't afford to go without pay."

"Consider tonight a paid vacation." Last night they'd taken in enough money to keep the place afloat another week. She'd locked the money in the trunk of her car with the intent of opening another tavern account. However, when she'd arrived, she began to have doubts. Last night, she'd half thought she could fix her mixed-up family and maybe save the tavern. But as she looked around the kitchen and saw how much needed to be done, she wasn't so sure all this was salvageable.

But she could make things right with Gannon.

And that's exactly what she intended to do right now.

Gannon's nerves danced with anger and frustration as he stared at the open case file on his desk. He needed to reread his old notes and look for similarities. But each time his mind got a hold of a sentence, he thought of Darcy.

Damn.

Darcy and Stephen.

It wouldn't surprise him if the two had been working together all along. It would be Glass's style to send in his girlfriend to do his dirty work. Gannon chaulked up this mistake to a libido that had gone far too long without servicing.

There was a knock at the door. He cursed it and then ignored it.

"I know you are in there," Darcy shouted. "I saw you go in."

He flipped a page in the file and tried to concentrate on another. "Get lost."

"Sorry, no can do. I'm going to stay out here until you answer." He imagined her eyes blazing.

He could be stubborn, too. "You're going to get very tired then."

"No chance. I closed the restaurant for the day so the way I figure it I got all the time in the world to sit on your doorstep and harp."

He would block her out. Concentrate. He needed to concentrate.

"I'm still here," she said. "Still, waiting."

Gannon smacked his hands on the table, got up and crossed the room. He yanked open the door. She stood there, leaning against the doorjamb. She was smiling, without the least bit of repentance in her eyes.

Her arms were crossed accentuating full breasts under the T-shirt. Her shirt was still inside out. "Your shirt is still inside out."

She glanced down at the raw seam. "So it is."

"What do you want?"

"You and I need to talk."

"Did your boyfriend send you here to pump me for more information?"

"Stephen *was* my boyfriend. Past tense. Believe me, he is the last person I wanted to see ride into town today—or any other day. The editor I called left his door open. Another reporter overheard the conversation and tipped Stephen off."

"Some friend."

"The D.C. reporting waters are full of sharks." Her eyes clouded with sadness and for a moment he almost invited her in. Almost.

"Look, I'm sorry I didn't tell you about Stephen. I knew you didn't like him."

A stray curl fell in the center of her forehead and he had the urge to brush it away.

"Despise might be a better word."

"Believe me, I know he can be a real jerk."

If she was lying, she was an excellent actress. "You don't have to explain anything to me."

"Can I come in?"

She leaned forward. Her nipples pressed against

her shirt and every sane thought in his head vanished. "Sure." His voice sounded ragged.

He summoned enough brain cells to step aside so she could enter his apartment. She turned and faced him and the light from the window behind her caught the highlights in her hair. He thought about the bed in his room, sheets rumpled. He wanted to see her on those sheets now, naked. He stepped toward her. If he had the sense God gave a tree stump he'd cut her loose now. She was trouble. He didn't need to be a part of her career breakthrough or her family problems.

"I still want to help you catch Nero," she said. "In fact, after that school fire, I want to catch him more than ever."

"Nero is still one good story." Bitterness dripped from each word.

"I don't care about the story anymore. This is bigger than a byline." Her voice sounded rusty, full of emotion.

"I could almost believe you."

Her lips were so full. They'd tasted so good. He shoved out a breath, stepped aside and let her into his apartment. He wanted her. There was no denying that. But sex with Darcy wouldn't be about love or commitment. It would be about need.

And maybe if he said that a few hundred times more he'd believe it.

She walked past him. Her gaze settled on the case files. "Did you find anything to help?"

"No. I know every detail by heart."

She faced him. "When do you think Nero will set another fire?"

"He's going to lay low for at least the rest of today, maybe even tomorrow. But he's moving much faster than I ever realized he would."

"How do you know?"

God, but he was so tired of Nero running his life. He didn't want to think about death, arson or destruction. He wanted to feel alive, if only for a couple of hours. "He'll be frustrated that today didn't go like he wanted. He'll need to regroup."

Worry lines deepened his brow. "Stephen thinks you could be Nero."

He moved closer. They were only six inches apart and he could feel the heat from her body and smell the smoke clinging to her hair. "Do you?"

She didn't speak for a moment. "At first I wasn't sure. The fires followed you here."

He refused to defend or justify. "And now?"

A heavy silence hung between them for a moment. "You're not Nero."

"Are you sure about that?"

She met his direct gaze. "Yes."

Gannon wanted to be inside Darcy. He wanted to feel her naked breasts pressed against his chest. "I don't want to talk about the fires right now."

Something in his voice had her eyes darkening. Her cheeks flushed. "I thought we decided that wasn't very professional."

He laid his hand on her shoulder. Her skin was like spun silk. "You're right, it's not."

She moistened her lips. "I should leave." But she stood rooted in her spot.

"You could." If she stayed, he wanted her to want this as much as he did. "Or you could stay." He captured the hem of her shirt. "And turn that shirt around."

Her fingers brushed his as she took hold of the hem. For a moment, she hesitated, as if warring inside herself. Then she grabbed hold of the fabric and pulled the shirt over her head. Slowly, she let the shirt fall to the floor.

His breath caught in his throat as he stared at her. Creamy, full breasts crowned a lacy bra. He leaned forward and kissed her, praying he had the strength to make this moment last.

As their lips touched, a soft mew formed in her throat. She wrapped her arms around his neck. His erection pressed against the fabric of her pants as his hand came up to cup her breast.

Her hands slid down his back and over his buttocks. She squeezed pressing him against her.

He broke the kiss but instead of speaking, he took her by the hand and pulled her toward his bed.

She didn't seem to notice. Again, she kissed him. Again, he prayed he didn't explode. He broke the kiss long enough to take off his own shirt. She kicked off her flip-flops.

Gannon reached for the clasp of her bra; undid it. He sucked in a breath as he stared at taut, pink nipples. His hands slid to the cotton waistband of her pants and undid the one button then gingerly eased the zipper down. He slid his hand under the pink cotton panties and cupped her tight buttocks then pulled it all off her.

Having her naked next to him shattered his will-power. He'd like to have taken it slowly, but his patience snapped.

Kissing her, he eased her back until she sat down on the edge of the bed. She scooted back toward the middle, her gaze locked on him.

He ditched his pants and came down on top of her covering her naked body with his. She opened her legs slightly, letting his erection press against her center. He kissed the hollow of her neck and then her taut nipple. He suckled one as he cupped the other.

Darcy arched, pressing her body against his. He snaked his hand down her belly to her moist center. He touched her and she hissed a breath between her teeth. "Unless you want this over before it starts, slow down, cowboy. I'm about ready to explode as is."

"Join the club." He had enough sense to reach into his nightstand for condoms. God knew how old the damn things were. Ripping open the foil package, he said a silent prayer of thanks that it hadn't rotted in the package. He slipped it over his erection.

Darcy opened her legs, rubbing her hands up his thigh. He pushed into her and she tightened around him.

Gannon's sliver of control vanished and he began to move inside her. She wrapped her legs around his waist and pulled him deeper.

He reached for her center and began to rub. Immediately, her body tensed and within seconds she dropped her head back, her body rigid with her climax.

The sight of her sent Gannon over the edge. He exploded inside of her and collapsed against her.

They lay there for several moments before he rolled off her. His eyes closed, savoring the total relaxation and sense of peace, knowing full well neither would last.

Darcy felt limp and knew she couldn't stand right now even if someone were ready to pay her ten thousand dollars. She'd never felt such a sense of completeness, such serenity.

Gannon sat up in bed. "I've water or soda in the fridge if you're thirsty."

"Soda."

"Be right back."

He rose from the bed, pulled on his jeans and left the room. Soda or water. Hardly romantic but then she'd be just a little foolish to expect any endearments from Gannon. They'd known each other, what, three days?

She rolled onto her stomach and buried her face in the pillow that still held his scent. She could count on one hand the number of men she'd slept with and all the others had had to work hard to win her.

But Gannon had looked at her and she'd fallen into bed with him.

When she heard his footsteps, she rolled back over and grabbed a sheet. Stupid to worry about modesty now, but without the desire pumping in her blood she felt exposed.

He came in the room. He wore only his jeans, his bare feet peeking out from the frayed hem. His chest was covered in a thick mat of hair that tapered all the way down over his flat belly to his jeans.

Her blood started to pump harder and she found herself wanting him all over again.

His fingers brushed hers as he handed her the soda. She drank it, praying the cold liquid would clear her mind. It tasted good, quenched her thirst but didn't cool her desire.

She rose up on her knees, letting the sheet drop, and looked up at him. His gaze was locked on hers. His breathing had grown shallow and if she didn't miss her guess, he had another erection. She took his soda from him, placed both on the nightstand and moved to him on her knees.

Kissing his flat belly, she let her hands wander down to the snap on his pants. She unfastened them and slid her hands inside.

A sigh shuddered through Gannon and he fell down on top of her, trapping her under his body. She let herself go to the sensations.

Nero struck a match and let it drop to the ground at his feet. He watched the flame dance and flicker out.

He lit another match.

Then another.

He was frustrated, angry and oddly very pleased with Gannon. He was a worthy opponent. The game was more interesting than he'd ever imagined.

Gannon had won today's battle, but later tonight he wouldn't be so lucky.

At first he'd been enraged to see Gannon and that woman show up at the school. When the fire alarm had blared, he'd nearly run from his hiding place in a fit of anger.

But he hadn't. He'd kept his composure.

In retrospect, he realized the courier must have arrived earlier than he was supposed to.

No wonder America was going to hell in a handbasket. Even couriers couldn't carry out simple instructions.

But later tonight there would be no lucky breaks. He would handle all the details himself.

Nothing was going to stop his next fire.

Nothing.

Chapter 12

Darcy woke with a start. The room was no longer bright but bathed in shadows. For an instant she wasn't sure where she was. And she didn't care. She felt wonderfully relaxed and more at peace than she had in years.

And then she remembered the afternoon she'd spent with Gannon.

She sat up in bed, shoving her curly hair out of her eyes. Swinging her legs over the side of the bed, she clicked on a nightstand light. An alarm clock read six-twelve. She'd slept the afternoon away.

Gannon wasn't in bed with her. Her gaze darted around the room. "Gannon?"

No answer.

He was gone.

"Great. Just great." He'd risen and left, no doubt hoping she'd be gone when he returned.

Worry and irritation replaced the peace. "I shouldn't have slept with him." There was so much riding on catching Nero and she'd wasted the afternoon in bed with Gannon. No doubt Gannon had recognized their mistake as well. "Nice going, Darcy."

Glancing at her naked body, she groaned. Clothes. She needed clothes. She spotted her top on the floor and had to root in the sheets for her bra and pants with her cell phone still attached.

She pulled on her top and had one leg in her pants when her cell phone started to ring. The noise caught her by surprise and she nearly tipped back onto the bed. She opened it without checking the number, half hoping it was Gannon.

"Hello?" she said.

"Darcy!" her mother said.

Darcy's shoulders immediately straightened. Could this moment get any worse? "Mom." She braced ready to be reamed out for closing the tavern tonight.

"Where are you?"

"Out. What do you need?" Pulling up her pants, she found one flip-flop under the bed and the second by the door. How it got there, she had no clue.

"I need your help." Her mother's voice trembled when she spoke."

"What's wrong?"

"It's Trevor. He came by this afternoon." She sounded so shaky.

Darcy sighed. "I know. I know. He's mad that I didn't open tonight."

"I don't think he even noticed."

Her mother wasn't mad at her. Something was wrong. "Then, what's the problem?"

"He's furious that you took last night's receipts. He said he needed the money. Said he was desperate." She let out a long shuddering sigh. "I've never seen him this angry. Darcy, he threw a whiskey bottle against the wall. Then he went for my purse. I told him to stay out of my wallet but he knocked me down and took what I had anyway."

Rage pumped through Darcy's veins. "Where is he now?"

"I don't know." She started to cry softly.

"Don't worry, Mom," she soothed. "I'll be right there."

"I don't know what to do," her mother said.

"I'll take care of everything." She closed the phone and headed down the stairs.

There was no sign of Gannon in the shop, confirming her worries. Still, she paused at his workbench to leave him a note that explained her situation. She wasn't sure if he cared one way or the other at this point, but she'd be honest with him, on the off chance he did care.

Darcy turned the lock and closed the door behind her. She jammed the note in the front door of his garage and headed over to the tavern.

Nero watched Darcy Sampson leave the note in Gannon's front door. Immediately, he was intrigued and surprised. It made sense that Gannon would need a woman from time to time but he'd never have pegged those two together. It explained why she was at the fire today and why the tavern was closed.

Ah, love. It was a wonderful thing.

Glancing from side to side, he strolled across the street, grabbed the note and replaced it with a pack of Rome matches before continuing on down the street. When he was a half block away, he read it: *Mom called. Trevor is in trouble again. Sorry. Call me. D.*

Nero moved to the shadows. He folded the note neatly and tucked it in his pocket.

Darcy added an interesting wrinkle to the game. She wasn't supposed to be a part of all this. That was too bad. He'd liked her. And had even thought about the possibility of more between them.

Closing his eyes, he imagined Darcy lying naked in a bed of red satin sheets, her hair tossed wildly on the pillows. And then the sheets turned to flames. She started to scream as her hair and skin melted into her bones. He was erect.

Darcy wasn't supposed to be a part of this game, but she was now.

And very soon she would burn.

★ ★ ★

Gannon didn't see the pack of matches at first.

Balancing burgers and sodas in one hand, he dug his keys out of his pocket with the other. He dropped his keys and cursed and then bent down to pick them up. He didn't expect to be gone from Darcy this long. He'd wanted to be back when she woke.

He smiled when he thought about her lying next to him in his bed. Nothing had felt so right in a very long time.

Smiling, he fumbled with the keys until he found the right one and then shoved it in the lock. That's when he saw the matches.

He froze and then glanced up toward his darkened bedroom. Darcy was alone, sleeping. And the bastard had been here.

Panic sliced through him. Tossing the burgers and sodas in a trash can, he quickly opened the door. He took the back staircase two at a time and burst into his bedroom. Darcy was gone.

A moment's panic overtook him. Dark thoughts raced through his mind. Had Nero done something to her?

He hurried to his window that overlooked the

tavern and reached for the phone. It was then that he saw Darcy standing in the dining room of the Varsity. She was drinking coffee with her mother. She was smiling.

The moment's relief gave way to anger. She'd left. No note. No thank you. No kiss my ass. Nothing.

What did you expect? She's a reporter, he scolded himself.

Darcy listened as her mother detailed her encounter with Trevor. "I told you, Mom, he needs help. He's just like Dad."

Her mother raised a shaking hand to the ice pack on her bruised forehead. "Darcy, it's not that bad."

She struggled to keep her voice even. "Mom, he knocked you down. He took your money. He's not your sweet baby Trevor when he needs a fix. He's an animal."

Her mother winced. "Don't talk about your brother that way."

"I'm not saying it to be hateful. Trevor needs help."

Her mother looked lost. "I don't even know where that kind of help would be."

"We'll figure it out together, okay? My guess is the county has some kind of program."

Her mother dabbed her red-rimmed eyes with a tissue. "The county? I just don't think we need to take such a drastic step. I mean contacting the county…what if they put it on our records?"

Darcy laughed though there was no mirth in it. "Mom, it's not like there's a huge permanent record out there that Big Brother keeps on us. There are just social workers willing to help."

She started to pace. "I…I can't do it. I can't turn my baby in."

"You're not turning him in. You are getting him help."

Mrs. Sampson's eyes snapped with anger. "No! And let's just leave it at that. Trevor had a bad day, is all. He will be better in the morning."

Darcy watched her mother walk out of the room. Frustrated, she went into the kitchen and opened the freezer and pulled out a two-gallon tub of chocolate ice cream. She set the container on the counter and dug a spoon out of the drawer. After scooping a generous spoonful, she put it in her mouth.

It tasted bland, too cold. She took another bite and then another. She was digging out her fifth bite when she realized she was eating just for the sake of it. Ice cream wasn't going to fix her family or whatever it was she had with Gannon. It was simply going to make her fat.

She covered the carton and shoved it back in the freezer.

Darcy pulled her cell phone off her waistband and dialed Paul's number. It was past seven, but she suspected he'd be there. Work was about all she had at this moment.

Paul picked up the call on the second ring. "Paul Tyler."

"Paul, it's Darcy. I called to see what you had for me."

Paul's chair squeaked as she leaned forward. "I heard you had another fire down there."

Darcy gripped the phone so tightly her knuckles turned white. "Did Stephen tell you?"

He hesitated. "Glass. How the hell would he know?"

"Barbara called him."

She heard Paul rise from his desk and slam his door closed. "Sorry."

"We can still be first on this." She went to the counter and pulled a pencil and pad of paper out of the drawer. "What can you tell me about the fires?"

Papers rustled in the background. "There have been two sets of fires like the ones you described. The first set was nine months ago in Dallas, Texas. A restaurant and warehouse burned. Both fires were fast burning and clearly arson. Cases never solved. The second set was outside of Detroit. An abandoned school and a restaurant. No fatalities in any of these cases."

Darcy wrote down all the information. She didn't see a pattern but maybe Gannon would. "Thanks."

"Do you think we've got a story?"

"Yes. I'm more convinced than ever that Nero is alive. The trick is finding him."

"Be careful."

"I will."

She hung up and dialed Gannon's number. Whatever there was or wasn't between them, they had a killer to catch. They could sort out their romance or lack thereof after Nero was caught.

The phone rang four times but there was no answer. The answering machine picked up. She didn't want to leave a message. Disconnecting, she walked to the front of the tavern. There were no lights on in his place.

An hour ago, she'd felt so at home in his loft apartment. Now she'd never felt more alone.

News of the school fire was on the front page of the local paper the next morning. The article referenced the other fires, but the writer didn't say anything about Nero or serial arsonists. However, it was just a matter of time. Soon the panic would begin. Nero would have the citizens of the small city afraid to enter any public building.

When Gannon arrived early at the chief's office this time, the receptionist smiled and stood immediately. "Mr. Gannon, the chief is expecting you."

He nodded. "Thanks."

The chief came to his feet the instant Gannon entered. Also in the room were the police chief and three fire captains dressed in their white shirts and dark blue uniform pants. They all shook hands.

When they sat, the chief said grimly, "I'm sorry I wasn't a better listener yesterday. But I think we will all agree that whether it's the real Nero or an imposter, we have a serial arsonist on our hands."

Gannon pulled the matches from his pocket and tossed them on the chief's desk. "These were stuck in my front door last night."

The chief opened the flap and read the bold handwriting. "*Next time you won't be so lucky.* What's he mean?"

Tension banded around Gannon's chest. "He knows I got lucky yesterday. The boy who delivered the clue yesterday wasn't supposed to drop it off until after one o'clock. But he had a class and a date that he didn't want to miss so he dropped it off early."

"You mean we have a horny boy to thank?" one of the captains asked.

Gannon nodded. "And Darcy Sampson. I didn't know where the school was. She found it for me. She pulled the fire alarm."

"My kid goes to that school," one of the fire-fighters said.

Chief Wheeler leaned forward. "What do you propose we do, Gannon?"

Gannon hated the idea of dealing with Nero again. But he'd see it through until Nero was caught for real this time. "Nero is moving faster. But his burn pattern is holding true. The next fire will be a church."

"How do we know he'll stick to the pattern? He's already changed his timetable," the chief said.

Gannon wished he had a crystal ball. "I don't know anything for certain. Everything I'm giving you is my best educated guess."

The chief sighed. "It's the best we got. Do you know which church might be in danger?"

"No."

"There must be over thirty churches in the area."

"It will be a visible target," Gannon said. "Nero has our attention now and he knows it. He'll want to keep the tension high." He turned to the police chief.

"Maybe we should go public and try to flush him out," the police chief said.

Gannon shook his head. "We tried that in D.C. I challenged him. He responded by burning a warehouse. Two people were killed." He was still haunted by those deaths.

"We can't just sit here," the police chief said.

Gannon met his gaze. "Get a list of all the churches in the area and we need to start searching them now."

"That's a needle in a haystack," the chief said.

"Exactly."

Gannon spent the night tossing and turning and the better part of the day working with the fire department. They searched a dozen churches, starting with the oldest ones in the city and working out from there. They found nothing.

His back ached and his head felt like it weighed a hundred pounds. He headed up to his apartment and flipped on the lights. He glanced toward his bedroom and the rumpled sheets of his bed. Thoughts of Darcy swirled in his head. He'd managed to push her out of his mind most of the day, but now she was everywhere. Her half cup of coffee still sat on the counter of his kitchen and the barest hint of perfume still lingered.

He jabbed his fingers through his hair. Making love to Darcy had been beyond his expectations. And it wasn't just the sex. When he'd woken yesterday and seen her lying beside him, something inside of him changed. Until her, he'd been content with his solitude. He'd welcomed the silence. Now he just felt alone.

He should have called her, found out why she'd left. But a part of him simply didn't want to know that last night was more about business than pleasure for her.

"You're a damn fool, Gannon." He strode to his answering machine. Its light blinked four messages. Sighing, he hit Play.

"Gannon, this is Stephen Glass. How about we get together on this arson thing? Could be good for both of—"

Gannon hit Delete. The second message was from Glass as was the third. He deleted both. As the fourth message started to play, he turned and walked toward the kitchen. "Hey, this is Darcy.

Sorry I missed you this morning. Call me." She hesitated. "I've got information from Paul."

Darcy. Shoving out a sigh, he headed over to the tavern. It was almost six and the place was nearly deserted. As he walked in the front door, he found her behind the bar. Even from here he could see she was tired. Her hair was pulled high on her head and dark circles smudged under her eyes.

He held the door for two customers that were leaving and then strode into the bar. She'd not seen him come in and her back was to him when he reached the bar.

"Have a seat," she said. "I'll be with you in a minute. She reached through the window to the kitchen and took two orders from the cook. When she turned and saw him, she nearly dropped her plates.

Gannon met her gaze. "Figured I could snag a soda."

She looked annoyed. "Regular or diet?"

The edge to her voice stirred his anger. He sat at the bar. "Regular."

"Give me a minute." She delivered the plates and seated another customer. She filled a glass with soda from the tap and set it in front of him. "I've been waiting on a call back from you all day. I have news from Paul."

It always came back to work with her. "Go ahead."

Darcy dug a piece of notepaper from her pocket and read to him about the fires. "If we could find someone in town who's been to Dallas and Detroit, we might have Nero."

He sipped his soda. "A needle in a haystack."

"Not really. I think Nero is in your life. I think he is someone you talk to everyday."

"Maybe."

"Make a list of your friends and acquaintances and I can start checking backgrounds."

"I'll do it."

She seated two new customers and took their drink orders while they read the menu. Returning to the bar, she poured a chardonnay and mixed a Scotch and soda. Once she'd delivered the drinks, she met his gaze. "So where do you think he'll strike next?"

"This on the record?" He heard the bitterness in his own words.

She frowned. "Only if you want it to be."

It all came down to trust. "I don't. And this includes leaking info to Glass."

She folded her arms. "I told you, Stephen and I are over."

It surprised him how much he wanted to believe that—how much he wanted to trust her. "If Nero holds to the pattern, he'll hit a church next. We've spent the better part of the day checking out local churches for traces of tampering."

"Anything?"

There was an edge about her that made his temper flare. "No."

Suddenly, she shook her head. "You know what? I could spend the next twenty minutes dancing around last night, but I'm too tired to play games. Where were you when I woke up?"

He'd be damned if she'd put him on the defensive. "I had to run out."

"Why didn't you call me today?"

"Why should I?"

She shrugged. "Oh, I don't know. Common courtesy, maybe? I woke up and you weren't there. So I left you a note and asked you to give me a call.

I mean, I'm not expecting you to marry me, but would a call have killed you?"

He set his glass down. His anger softened. "I never got the note."

Her bluster faded a bit. "How could you not get it? I taped it to your front door. You couldn't have missed it."

"It wasn't there." He sipped his drink, pleased she hadn't just taken off. "So what did the note say?"

"My mom called. More stuff with Trevor."

He kept his tone neutral. "He all right?"

She looked so damn tired, weary. "That's another story, another day."

He'd been walking around all day long, annoyed for no reason. He wanted to touch her now and take her back to bed. "There were matches from Nero on my door."

"What?"

"He's close, Darcy, very close."

Her face paled. "We need to find him fast. What if he gets tired of the game and turns on you?"

"I don't think he would." He frowned as a thought occurred to him. "But you need to be careful."

The connection between them had returned. And she wasn't going to stand here and pretend it hadn't.

Coming around the bar, she came up to him. He stood and unable to resist, took her in his arms. Without hesitating he kissed her. Her lips softened immediately and she wrapped her arms around his neck.

"When do you close tonight?" His voice sounded rough.

"Ten."

He kissed her on the forehead and reluctantly stepped back. "I'll be back then."

"Okay." She closed her eyes and leaned her forehead against his shoulder. "I spent all day being mad at you and a couple of words and one kiss and I melt. You've gotten under my skin, Gannon."

He rubbed his hand up her arm. "Be careful. If Nero knows you are with me, you are in danger."

She hadn't considered that angle. "I can take care of myself."

"That's what my ex-wife said." His jaw tensed as he relived the memories. "She worked in a clothing store. One afternoon, the Dumpster behind the store caught fire. The smoke was thick and poured into the store. Amy was overcome by smoke. Two patrons were taken to the hospital with smoke inhalation problems. The fire was ruled an accident but Amy and I both knew it was Nero."

"I'm sorry."

"That fire was her breaking point. She'd endured months of me working long hours and when I was home, I was always in a foul mood. She couldn't take it anymore. She left the next day."

"I'm sorry. But I'm not running. I'm not afraid."

"You should be."

Chapter 13

It was after 2:00 a.m. when Darcy woke, unexpectedly. She lay in Gannon's bed. He lay on his side, his body spooned against her, his arm draped over her waist. For a moment, she laid perfectly still, listening to his deep breathing, savoring his scent.

But a restlessness took root and she found she had to get up. Gingerly, she moved his arm off her and slid out of the bed. She grabbed a blanket from the edge of the bed and went to the window.

Darcy stared out at the full moon. Endless stars winked in the night sky. She hated it when she couldn't sleep. In the quiet of the night, worries and doubts had a tendency to come to life.

She rested her head against the pane of glass. Tonight her worries were not over family or deadlines but over Gannon. She'd known the man only a few days and she'd not only been to bed with him twice, but she was falling for him. Hard.

Her actions were not those of the analytical woman who guarded her trust and love so closely.

She heard Gannon's footsteps and despite her misgivings smiled as he wrapped his strong arms around her waist and pulled her against his hard chest.

Bolts of desire shot through her. She swallowed, praying she didn't just melt right here in front of him. "I thought you were asleep."

"I was. Then I realized you were gone and I wanted to find you."

"I'm glad you did."

"You have the most beautiful skin," he said. "I never get tired of touching you."

Words failed her. Closing her eyes, she savored the feel of his fingertips. Outside, the moon glistened bright.

He tugged her closer, molding their bodies together. He kissed her on the soft skin below her jaw. The dark stubble of his beard teased her senses. Breathing suddenly seemed difficult as if the air had vanished from the room.

"You are trouble, Gannon," she whispered as she faced him.

He laughed as his hands entwined in her hair, he guided her head back so that her lips tipped up to his. He kissed her hard, communicating all the desire and passion in his body.

She could have sworn the floor shifted under her feet as she savored the kiss.

"Lose the blanket," he murmured. "I want to see you."

She let go of the blanket and it fell from her shoulders and pooled at her feet. He cupped her breasts and coaxed her nipples into hard peaks.

"Gannon, you drive me crazy," she said, her voice hoarse.

"Good." He led her back to the bed.

As she leaned back on the bed, she expected explosive passion as they'd shared earlier this evening. In fact, she welcomed it. She liked losing herself in desire. But when Gannon covered her body with his, he was in no rush. He kissed her shoulder, her collarbone and then her lips. The tenderness caught her by surprise.

Her hands skimmed his muscled back as he kissed her on the lips. He rose up and moved down to kiss her nipples. She sucked in a breath when he kissed her flat belly.

When she lay naked before him he straddled her hips. He stared down at her, his eyes alight with passion. Then he leaned forward and began to kiss her breasts, taking his time as he suckled each.

Darcy arched her back. She wanted him to hurry, wanted the release he'd given her earlier. But Gannon was in no rush this time.

He kissed the hollow of her neck and then captured her lips again. He continued to fondle and kiss her until she thought she'd go out of her mind. "Gannon, if you don't do something now, I'm going to lose my mind."

He chuckled, then pressed his naked body against hers. She was so ready for him. She opened her legs wide. She wasn't one for begging but she was on the verge when he slid inside her. Slowly he began to move inside of her, savoring every thrust.

When his fingers touched her moist center, she couldn't hold back anymore. Desire and release exploded as she called out his name. Her climax was too much for Gannon and he began to move faster and faster inside her. Within seconds, he tumbled over into the sweet abyss with her.

Darcy was quite certain every bone in her body had melted. She couldn't have moved now if she'd tried.

Gannon rolled toward her on his side and pulled her into a tight embrace. He kissed her on the side of the neck and fell into a deep sleep.

As Darcy drifted closer to sleep, she wondered what she was going to do with this complicated man she was rapidly falling in love with.

Across town, Nero whistled as he sprinkled gasoline around the messy apartment. He inhaled, savoring the scents.

He felt almost like a parent welcoming a new offspring into the world as he dumped the last of the gas on the couch and set the can down. He surveyed the high ceilings and the detailed crown molding. He loved the older buildings like this one. They had such style, such beauty and they burned so easily.

Nero reached in his pocket for a pack of Rome matches. He struck the match and watched the flame dance on the end of the stick before tossing it onto the floor. Immediately, the place was ablaze. The fire snaked across the floor engulfing the couch and the wall behind it.

Nero took a step back, pleased by the way the fire danced up the wall and to the ceiling. The oxygen grew thin as the fire sucked it all in.

Soon his child would consume the building. Soon, it would all be destroyed.

The phone rang in Gannon's apartment at two forty-two in the morning. He woke with a start. Darcy lay on her side facing him, her arm tossed recklessly over his chest. He patted her arm as he snatched up the phone. "Yeah."

"It's Chief Wheeler. We just got a call on another fire. I'm headed there now."

Gannon shrugged off the sleep coating his brain. "A church?"

Darcy woke, lifting her head. Sleep dulled her gaze. She switched on the bedside light on her side.

"No, an apartment."

The tone of Gannon's voice had Darcy's attention. She sat up, clutching the sheets to her breasts.

Gannon ran his fingers through his hair. "This doesn't make sense."

"It's Trevor Sampson's place."

He glanced at Darcy. She'd rubbed the sleep from her eyes and looked completely alert. "Damn."

"You know what this means?" In the background, the fire truck's siren blared.

"What does it mean?"

"Trevor Sampson is Nero, or at least a poor copycat."

Gannon's stomach tightened. "None of this makes sense, Chief."

"Makes perfect sense to me," the chief said.

Trevor reminded Gannon less of Nero and more of Raymond Mason, the man Nero had set up last year. "I'll be right over." He hung up the phone.

Darcy frowned. "What happened?"

A year ago, he'd have sprung out of bed and dashed to the fire without a moment's hesitation or a thought to what he was leaving behind. Then the chase had been everything. Now he resented it. He didn't want to leave Darcy.

"There's been another fire. It was just called in." With an effort, he switched on a light, rose and collected his pants from the floor.

She scrambled out of bed and started to search for her clothes. She found her jeans tossed casually over a chair next to his shirt. "I'm coming with you."

He pulled on his pants and zipped them up. "It's Trevor's apartment."

"What?" She stood naked, her clothes gathered in her hands.

She dumped the clothes on the bed and pulled her shirt over her head. "Where's Trevor?"

"No one knows."

She slid her jeans on. "Do you think Trevor is Nero?"

He crossed the room toward her and knelt in front of her. "No. But that doesn't mean he didn't set fire to his apartment. Profit is the number one motive for arson."

She shook her head. "None of this makes sense."

He didn't like what he was going to have to say. "It does to the chief. I can already tell you what he's going to say. Trevor has got a drug problem, his tavern is in trouble and with me in town, it would make sense to resurrect Nero."

"No. Trevor can be an idiot but he's not an arsonist."

"Drugs and booze change people. He would have slugged you the other night if I hadn't been there to stop him."

Her eyes filled with tears. "He didn't mean it."

He brushed away a tear falling down her face. "I didn't say I believed this. But the chief will. And if Glass gets ahold of the story, he's going to run with it."

"Oh, God."

"Let's get over to Trevor's."

"Okay."

Minutes later, they were on Gannon's bike speeding through the night. The air was cool, the sky clear and bright. A thousand stars winked above. Darcy's warm body pressed against his. Any other night, he'd have enjoyed the ride.

They arrived at Trevor's apartment within minutes. The building was engulfed in flames. Three fire trucks were at the scene, hoses extended, water shooting at full blast. Smoke poured from ventilation holes made by breaking the basement apartment windows.

One glance and he knew the building would be a total loss. The fire had eaten through the structure, destroying everything it touched.

According to Darcy, the building was Victorian and had been converted into apartments years ago. Trevor's place was in the basement. A basement fire was one of the hottest fire situations. For the firefighters, it would be like maneuvering down a chimney into a roaring fire.

On the street across from the burning building, three families stood in their pajamas. One woman, wearing a blue bathrobe, sobbed openly. All stared in shock at the blaze as everything they owned was consumed.

"My God," Darcy murmured.

Chief Wheeler, wearing his fire gear, strode toward them. He glanced at Darcy and then at Gannon. He was clearly surprised by her presence.

Gannon's jaw tightened. Darcy was staying and if the chief wanted a fight, he'd give it to him.

The chief looked exhausted as he shook Gannon's hand. "Darcy, do you know where your brother is?"

She shook her head. "No."

He frowned. "The police have put out an APB on him."

"Chief!" one of the firefighters shouted as he ran toward him. "We've got two people still unaccounted for. An elderly woman on the second floor."

The chief stared at the blaze as two firefighters stepped forward. They wore full gear, self-contained breathing apparatuses. "Make it quick."

The firefighters nodded and disappeared into the blazing front door of the building. The heat from the inferno burned Gannon's nostrils and warmed his skin.

An explosion echoed from the basement. Several people screamed and stepped back.

Gannon stood rigid. Nero had nearly killed two firefighters in D.C. He prayed these two men wouldn't die tonight.

Darcy clung to his arm, her body as rigid as wood. Tense seconds passed.

The firefighters came out of the front door of the building. One carried the old woman over his shoulder. The paramedics met the firefighters and took the woman whose white nightgown was covered in soot.

One of the firefighters staggered, clearly overcome by the heat.

The paramedics looked down at the woman. They started to work on her immediately, opening her airway and checking for a pulse. They loaded her into the back of the ambulance as one paramedic started CPR. The doors to the ambulance closed, its lights started flashing and it took off toward the hospital.

"Trevor didn't do this," Darcy whispered. "He's got his problems, but he wouldn't do something like this."

Gannon stared down at her. "We don't know that for certain."

Darcy hugged her arms around her chest. "I know. He wouldn't do this." Tears filled her eyes. "Do you think he got trapped in the fire?"

"I don't know."

"My mother is going to be devastated. She's barely holding it together as it is."

"It's going to be hours before the building cools enough for the firefighters to investigate."

"This is a nightmare."

Gannon laid his hand on her shoulder. "Let me take you home."

Helpless to do anything else, she nodded.

When Darcy finally got out of bed, it was past ten o'clock the next morning. Her head felt as if it were going to explode and her body was stiff. Gannon had dropped her off at 4:00 a.m. She'd then been faced with the grim task of telling her mother what had happened. She'd been up most of the night with her mother, trying to calm her.

Dressed in jogging pants and a T-shirt, she came downstairs, her running shoes still in hand. She went to the phone in the kitchen while she started a pot of coffee.

As the machine started to brew, she called the chief. His secretary put her through. "Darcy." His voice was terse and he sounded tired.

"Have you found Trevor?"

"No. The police are still looking for him."

"He didn't do this."

His answer was silence. "The arson crews, including Gannon, are at the apartment building now sifting through the remains of the building. We'll see what they come up with." His voice softened. "Hang in there, Darcy."

"Thanks." She hung up the phone.

The story that had started out so distant had turned very personal. A week ago, she'd pitied Raymond Mason's sister as she'd sat in the coffee shop and pleaded with Darcy to clear her brother's name. And now Darcy had become like Sara Highland, a woman desperate to prove her brother's innocence.

As she poured herself a mug of coffee, she heard a knock at the door. She looked up to see Stephen coming through the kitchen door. In the lock were her keys.

Stephen pulled them out and tossed them in the air before holding them out to her. "Darcy, I see you're still leaving your keys in the door. You're going to get yourself in trouble one day if you don't watch it. You never know who could come through that door."

She took the keys. He was the last person she wanted to see right now. "Thanks. What can I do for you?"

Stephen grinned. "Oh, I think you know. I want to talk to your brother."

"He's not here."

Stephen walked over to the coffee machine and poured himself a cup of coffee. "So baby brother thinks he'll try his hand at arson? Makes sense. I mean he must have known I'd been reporting on Nero in D.C. He was full of questions the last time he visited us in D.C. My guess is that he probably figured it was his chance to grab some limelight."

She knew Stephen's tactics. He wanted to stoke her temper so she'd speak without thinking. But she wasn't going to give him anything. "Take your coffee and leave, Stephen."

He took a sip. "You always did make the best cup of coffee." He glanced around the kitchen. "I can't picture you working here. Now I know why you were so tight-lipped about where you grew up."

"Leave, Stephen."

He shook his head. "Come on, Darcy. Throw me a bone here. Why do you think your brother set the fires? Money, kicks? I'm hearing rumors he had a drinking problem. Baby bro always could slam back the beers as I remember."

Her temper rose. "I'm not talking to you."

"Hey, I get that you think I'm on your turf. You came down here sniffing out a Nero lead. And Trevor is your brother. But we can share the glory, babe. Hey, with my contacts, I could get you a gig reporting at the television station."

She moved to the alley door and opened it. "Get out of here now or I'm calling the cops."

His smile faded. "No one knows if Trevor is the real Nero or just a cheap knockoff. Frankly, from what I've learned about him, I don't think he has the brains to pull off what Nero did in D.C." He leaned a fraction closer. "But Gannon does. Makes sense he'd set up a screwup like Trevor, just like he did that Mason guy in D.C."

Her back was ramrod straight. "Get out or I call the cops."

He set his cup down on the counter but made no move to leave. "What do both sets of fires have in common? Nero and Gannon. I'd bet my last dollar Gannon is Nero."

Anger singed her veins. "You are so wrong."

His eyes glistened. "The old lady they pulled out of the building died about an hour ago."

Darcy took a step back. She felt as if she'd been punched in the stomach. "My God."

Stephen closed the distance between them and laid his hands on her shoulders. "Whoever set that fire is a murderer. Come on, Darcy, work with me. Together we can solve this thing so that no one else dies."

Tears pooled in her eyes. The image of the woman lying so helplessly on the stretcher haunted her. "Get out."

"Darcy, please."

"Go, Stephen, just go."

"Darcy—"

"You heard the lady." Nathan entered the back door from the alley. Frowning, he glared at Stephen. "Hit the road."

Stephen didn't budge. "And who the hell are you, pal?"

Nathan moved to stand beside Darcy. He pulled

her behind him. "A friend. Now get out before I toss you out."

Stephen could be obnoxious and pushy but he hated violence. Even the threat of it always had him backing down. He moved toward the door. "This isn't over, Darcy. You know that. Let me help you."

She squared her shoulders. "You are the last person I'd ever ask for help."

Stephen grinned. "Never say *never*, Darcy." He strode out of the tavern leaving her seething.

She released a breath when the back door slammed closed. "It's beyond me what I ever saw in that man."

Nathan lifted an amused eyebrow. "Don't tell me you and Glass were an item?"

"Unfortunately, yes."

Nathan rubbed the back of his neck. "I only know the guy from television but it doesn't take much to realize that his number one priority is ratings."

"Tell me about it." She shrugged off her anger, refusing to let Stephen steal another minute of her day. "Thank you. I'd never have gotten rid of him if you hadn't showed up."

"No problem."

"So what brings you here?"

Nathan's stance was relaxed now. He wore his customary button-down shirt and khakis. Not a hair out of place. "Just wanted to let you know I'd be out of town for a few days."

"Oh, where are you headed?" She tried to sound interested but her thoughts drifted back to what Stephen had said.

"Down to North Carolina. There's some property on the coast that I might be interested in developing."

She willed herself to smile. "Hey, well, good luck. Maybe by the time you get back, we'll have this Nero mess sorted out."

Nathan frowned. "Somehow I don't think that is going to happen. Nero strikes me as very clever."

"Even clever people slip up."

"Gannon didn't catch him in D.C."

She found herself rising to Gannon's defense. "He's learned a few things since then. Nero won't get out of this one alive."

Nathan hesitated. "I heard what Glass said. What if he is right? What if Gannon is Nero?"

"He's not." The force behind her words made her sound more defensive than self-assured.

Nathan nodded. "I like Gannon, Darcy, but the truth of the matter is that I don't know him all that well."

"You two are friends."

"We've known each other a couple of years, swapped a few drinks and stories. But I can't tell you what makes the man tick."

"He's not Nero."

He laid his hand on her shoulder. "I like you and I don't want anything bad to happen to you." He leaned forward and kissed her on the cheek.

A chill snaked her spine. "I'll be fine."

Chapter 14

Nathan had not been gone five minutes when a courier arrived at Darcy's back door with a letter. "Darcy Sampson?" he asked.

"Yes?"

"I've got a note here from a Mr. Gannon. If you'll just sign here." He held out a pen and shoved a release slip toward her.

She studied the manila folder. "Why would he send a courier to deliver a letter to me?"

The courier scratched behind his ear. "Hey, lady, I don't know. I just need for you to sign the release form so I can get going. I got three other packages to deliver by noon."

She signed the form and took the envelope. She went to her purse to get a tip but he held up his hand. "Already been taken care of."

She smiled at Gannon's thoughtfulness.

When the courier left, she opened it. *Darcy, I know who Nero is. Meet me at the Riverton Baptist Church in an hour.*

She folded the note over and deepened the crease with her fingertip. *In an hour.* Why hadn't he told her who Nero was? Why the secrecy?

She had just enough time to go upstairs and check in on her mother. All the problems she and her mother had had over the years paled to this. Her mother, who'd seem so strong, now needed protection as if she were a child lost in the woods.

Nero was not going to destroy her family.

The end of the game was coming so fast that Nero had mixed emotions. Though he was eager to see how the story would play out, he was also sorry to see it end. Like a good book or a fine wine, he'd savored every bit, every sip.

He pulled out a book of Rome matches and ran his thumb over the raised gold lettering as he checked his watch. Any minute now, Darcy would be coming out of the tavern.

Three minutes later, she emerged right on time. She'd changed into jeans, a clean white shirt and she'd pulled her curls into a ponytail. She looked lovely.

He watched Darcy leave the tavern and climb into her black Corolla. She headed north toward Riverton Baptist Church.

There was so much to like about Darcy Sampson.

Smart, funny, bright, she had a lot to offer a man.

Too bad, she'd be dead in an hour.

Larry swung by the garage just after eleven o'clock. Gannon looked up from his files, annoyed at the interruption. He'd just returned from what remained of the apartment building. The investigators had found traces of accelerant that had been stockpiled in Trevor's apartment. They'd also gained access to his safety deposit box and found an envelope containing newspaper clippings that not only detailed the Preston Springs fires but the D.C.

ones, as well. However, they hadn't found Trevor's body. He was out there somewhere, alive.

Chief Wheeler and the other men were convinced that Trevor was their man, but Gannon was not sure of anything. This all reminded him too much of last year.

He'd just returned and planned to look over his files again. He knew in his gut that he was overlooking something. Something, like a forgotten name, was on the tip of his tongue.

"Gannon, you busy?" Larry asked, flashing his easy grin.

"Yeah."

Larry's gaze skimmed the files spread out on the workbench. "Well, I'll be quick."

Gannon considered tossing him out but decided to hear him out. Hammering away at these files certainly wasn't solving anything right now. "What do you need, Larry?"

"Got this lead on a motorcycle. An Indian. Vintage. Very sleek. The seller only wants three grand for it."

"And?"

"It's not exactly running."

"Kind of a sticking point in my book."

"I was hoping you'd come with me to have a look at it, maybe give me an idea of what it would cost to fix it."

"Can't do it today."

"Oh hey, no problem. The guy said he was in no rush. The guy lives in Charlottesville, not more than an hour from here."

Likely this guy had no buyers. Fixing an old bike wasn't cheap. "Great."

Larry reached in his pocket and pulled out a pack of cigarettes. He tapped out a single and put it in his mouth. "Are you still working on this fire thing?"

Fire thing. Gannon wasn't sure if he should laugh or be angry with Larry. The guy had reduced the decade's most notorious arsonist to a trivial blip. "Yeah."

Larry shrugged as he rooted in his pockets for a pack of matches. He came up empty in the first two. "Saw that Glass guy on TV. You think Trevor did it?"

"No."

"The guy is a mess but I don't think he'd set

fires." From his back pocket he pulled out a pack of matches.

Gannon was only half paying attention to Larry as he pulled out a match, struck it, and lit the tip of his cigarette.

However the smell of the smoke had him looking up. He'd been dying for a cigarette all morning. "Can I have one of those?"

Larry pulled out the pack of Marlboros and tossed them to Gannon. "Thought you gave it up."

He pulled out a cigarette and put it in his mouth. "I did."

Larry tossed the matches in his right hand a couple of times before he opened the flap and pulled out a match. As he raised the flame to Gannon's cigarette, the flicker of the book's red cover caught Gannon's eye.

Gannon blew out the match, pulled the cigarette out of his mouth and took the match from Larry. Rome matches. His blood ran cold. "Where did you get these?" Gannon's voice was little more than a hoarse whisper as he stared down at the red pack. For a moment his heart pounded in his chest and the hairs on the back of his neck stood up. Larry couldn't be Nero.

Larry sniffed. "I don't know. Around. I'm always losing matches, people are always giving them to me."

Gannon prayed for patience. "It's important, Larry. I need you to think. Think hard."

Larry cracked his knuckles. "Well, I've bummed matches off a couple of folks lately. There was the waitress at the truck stop outside of Richmond. The diner in Roanoke and Nathan gave me a pack the other night."

"Nathan? I didn't think he smoked."

"Yeah. I never figured him for a smoker either, but he confessed he likes a cigar now and then."

He ran his thumb over the pack of matches. Nathan had lived in D.C. during the last set of fires. Darcy had said there'd been similar fires in Dallas and Detroit over the last year.

Without a word to Larry, he went upstairs to his computer and Googled Braxton Development, Nathan's employer. The link to the company's Web site came up—in fact Nathan was profiled under the *Property Manager* button.

Nathan had worked for them as a property manager for twenty years. His projects had won building and design awards and he was considered one of the top executives in the company.

Gannon clicked *Developed Properties*. The list that appeared included properties in New York, Washington, San Francisco, Detroit and Dallas—with a new site planned for North Carolina. He'd bet his last dollar there were unexplained fires that matched Nero's MO in the other cities, as well.

For a moment, his mind raced and he couldn't think. Nathan was Nero.

He thought back to their first meeting at the gym. Nathan had sought him out. He'd been the one to strike up the friendship.

The more he thought about it the more it made sense. Nathan had sought him in D.C. Nathan had looked him up in Preston a month ago. Nathan had made friends with Chief Wheeler and he loved to hear stories about fires.

"You all right, man?" Larry asked from the doorway. "You look like you saw a ghost."

"I have." He reached for the telephone and called the chief.

"Gannon, what's up?" the chief said.

Gannon detailed his theories to the chief. "He needs to be picked up."

"Damn, he's a respected member of the community. The Braxton property is a huge boom to economic development."

Gannon's fingers tightened around the receiver. "Chief, Nathan is Nero. And if we don't move quickly, we are going to lose him."

Chief Wheeler was silent. "I'll have the police put out an APB on him. We'll bring in him for questioning."

Relief washed over Gannon. "Great. Thanks."

Larry scratched his head over the conversation he'd just heard. "Damn, you sure about all this?"

"Yes."

"Too bad, I liked that guy."

Bitterness rose in his throat. "He's a likable guy." He rose. "I've got to find Darcy."

"Oh yeah, right. She'll be glad to hear all this."

"Lock up on your way out."

"No problemo."

Gannon hurried down the stairs and across the street. Darcy needed to know—not only for Trevor's sake, but also for her own. As likable as Nathan Collier could be, Nero was a cold-blooded killer who could easily turn on her just for the sport of it.

He crossed the street and went to the tavern's front door. It was locked so he jogged around to the back alley door. The door was open and inside the kitchen there was a man standing by the island chopping up mounds of vegetables. Darcy had mentioned a cook named George.

"You George?"

"That's right."

"Have you seen Darcy?" Gannon asked.

The man looked at him briefly and then returned to his work. "She was rushing out of here when I arrived. Said she'd be back in a couple of hours."

"Did she say where she was going?"

George looked annoyed. "Said she was going to meet you."

His gut tightened. "Me? We had no meeting."

"Look, I ain't no social director. I don't know where she is. You two need to get your own schedules straight."

Gannon walked over to George, took the knife

from him and drove it into the counter next to the cook's hand. "You have no idea where she went?"

The irritation in George's brown eyes vanished when he locked gazes with Gannon. "She left a note on the bar for her mother."

Without a thanks, Gannon hurried into the tavern. On the bar was the note. He opened the letter. If he was wrong, he'd apologize later.

Mom,
I've gone to meet Gannon at the Riverton Baptist Church. I'll be back in time for dinner. Don't worry about Trevor. It's all going to be fine. Gannon and I are going to prove that he didn't do any of this. Love, Darcy.

Gannon crumbled the note in his hand. Riverton Baptist Church. Damn! Nero was going after Darcy.

"George!" he shouted, racing into the kitchen.

"Now what do you want?" he asked setting his knife down.

"Do you know where the Riverton Baptist Church is?"

"Sure. It's about ten miles from here out on 250."

"On the way to Gully's?"

"Just past it on the right."

Sweat trickled down his spine. "Call the fire department and the cops and tell them I said to get there as fast as they can. And call the church and tell them to clear the building."

"What for?"

"Do it!" he shouted, already turning toward the door. He raced across the street and hopped on his bike, praying he wasn't already too late to save Darcy.

Darcy entered the small church twenty minutes later. She'd first been in this church when she was a kid. Her mother had brought food for a Christmas food drive. She remembered the visit because it was one of the few days she and her mother had spent alone, away from her father, Trevor and the tavern. That day her mother had bought her a piece of stick candy and they'd gone to the drugstore and looked at makeup.

On that long-ago day, the church had been full of people and alive with activity. The choir's loft in the back of the sanctuary had been full of carolers. Children had run down the center aisle laughing as an army of women organized food baskets on temporary tables set up in the front of the church.

Now the place was eerily quiet. The overcast sky blocked most of the sun that should have been streaming through the tall, clear windows flanking the sides of the church. The overhead lights were off, save for the dim beam shining down on a large white cross, which hung above a simple altar.

Darcy walked down the center aisle past the twenty rows of wooden pews. This didn't feel right.

"Gannon?" Her voice bounced off of the white walls. "Gannon? Where are you?"

As she moved closer toward the altar, an odor drifted out toward her. One deep breath told her what it was—gasoline! She stopped by the first row of pews.

"Gannon!" In the answering silence she heard only her heartbeat. And then she heard a faint rustling sound.

"Darcy." The weak, slurred voice came from behind the altar.

She moved closer. "Trevor?"

"Darcy."

She raced around the altar. There she found Trevor slumped forward. He reeked of whiskey and his clothes were covered in soot.

Darcy knelt beside her brother. She cupped his chin in her hands and raised his face. "Trevor!" He could barely open his eyes, as he mouthed her name. Panic ignited in her. She'd never seen him this incapacitated.

"Oh God, Trevor, what have you done to yourself?"

He slowly shook his head. "I didn't do it. I didn't set the fire."

"Trevor, there is a mountain of evidence against you. The police are looking for you."

With seemingly great effort, he opened his eyes. "I didn't do it."

Darcy believed her brother. "I know."

As he slumped forward into unconsciousness, a distant sound caught her attention. It sounded like the roar of a wave rolling under her feet.

The hairs on the back of Darcy's neck rose. The noise grew louder as if a sleeping giant had awoken.

It was then that she smelled smoke and noticed the ghostly wisps rising from the air vents in the corner.

The basement beneath them was on fire.

Her hands trembling, she wrapped Trevor's limp arm around her neck. "Trevor, we've got to get out of here right now."

Trevor moaned but didn't open his eyes. He pushed her hand away as if he only wanted to sleep.

"Trevor!" she shouted. "Get up!"

He rolled his head from side to side. "Go away, Darcy. Let me sleep a few more minutes."

She smacked him hard across the face. "Get up!"

Sharp pain opened his eyes. "Leave me alone!"

Darcy tugged him up. "The building is on fire. We are going to die if we don't get out of here right now."

Underneath her feet, she felt the rumble of the fire. It was growing, eating through the building inch by inch.

Where was Gannon?

The back door to the church opened.

Sunlight streamed through the door, shadowing the face of the tall figure standing at the back of the church. "Gannon!"

"Sorry, babe," Stephen said stepping forward. "But will I do?" He laughed.

At this point Satan would have been welcome. "I need help with Trevor."

Stephen started down the aisle. "Trevor is up there?" His tone was lean and hungry. Darcy knew he tasted headlines.

"Yes, and he's not moving."

"I knew it!" he shouted. "I knew if I followed you, you'd lead me to the story."

For once she was grateful for Stephen's blind ambition. "I need help getting him out of the church. The basement is on fire."

Stephen stopped midway up the aisle. He glanced down at his feet as if he expected the floor to crumble beneath him. "Damn. Did Trevor set the fire?"

Frustration sliced through her composure. Smoke was starting to seep faster through the floorboards. "Can we get out of here and discuss this outside? The building is on fire."

He glanced back toward the door and then back at her. Clearly, self-preservation warred with getting the story. "I get an exclusive if I get him out of here."

"Fine."

He started to jog toward the altar. "The story is all mine, Darcy. You don't get credit. My crews are waiting outside to tape the interview."

The fire roared louder. "Fine! Now get over here."

Stephen reached down, grabbed Trevor by the collar and hauled him to his feet. "He smells like booze."

Darcy wrapped her arm around Trevor's midsection. "I think he's been drugged."

Stephen put his arm around Trevor. "Damn, he weighs a ton."

The trio started down the center aisle. They were halfway down when the door to the church slammed closed.

Stephen cursed. Without a word spoken, Darcy and Stephen hurried their pace toward the door.

Stephen tried the brass doorknob. "It's locked."

Sweat dampened the back of Darcy's shirt. "What?"

He released his hold on Trevor and tried the door

again. Jiggling it harder, he shoved his shoulder into the door. It didn't budge. "It's locked!"

Darcy couldn't support Trevor alone and was forced to lower him to the carpeted floor. She raised a trembling hand to her forehead.

The door was locked. The fire roared beneath them. She'd been summoned here unexpectedly. It all added up now. "Oh, God. We've been set up."

Stephen smacked his fist against the thick oak door. "What do you mean—set up?"

"I got a note from Gannon. He told me to meet him here."

"I told you that guy was trouble. He is Nero," Stephen shouted.

"Gannon isn't Nero." The growing smoke tightened her lungs, making breathing difficult now.

The fire bellowed in the basement. Floorboards creaked. Like a beast fully awake now, the fire was bent on one thing only—destruction.

Stephen pounded on the door. "Like hell he's not! The guy set us up!"

Heat rose up under their feet. They only had minutes before the floorboards gave way. "Gannon wouldn't do this to me. He wouldn't."

"Wise up, Darcy," he said coughing from the smoke. "The guy is insane. No doubt he has one of those dual personalities. One sets fires, the other puts them out."

Darcy's mind reeled with confusion and panic as Stephen ran to one of the tall windows along the wall. When he realized the window didn't open, he searched around frantically until he saw a baptismal font in the back of the church. He wrenched the marble bowl out of the stand, ran back to the window and shattered the glass with it. Without a backwards glance, Stephen jumped out the window.

Darcy ran to the window. The fresh air smelled so sweet. "Stephen, don't leave us."

Blood from the broken glass coated his hands as he rose from the thick grass to his feet. "I'll try the door from the outside."

Tense seconds passed. The fire growled. She heard Stephen on the other side of the door. He pounded briefly and then stopped.

When he reappeared at the window, panic tightened his face. "The door has been padlocked."

"What!"

"There's no way to open it."

"I can't get Trevor out alone."

He shook his head. "Save yourself. Jump."

"I can't leave him. You'll have to come in and help me get him out."

Stephen took a step back. "I'm not coming back in there."

"What?"

"Save yourself, Darcy."

Darcy glanced toward her brother and then back at Stephen. "I'm not leaving him."

From the shadows near the pulpit, she heard laughter. Darcy looked up and by the back exit saw a figure. "Gannon!"

More laughter echoed. "No." He stepped forward enough so that Darcy could see him clearly.

Nathan.

And she knew.

"Nero!" she shouted.

He nodded. "Yes."

"Why are you doing this?" The heat was building up. The smoke grew thicker.

He shrugged. "It's all part of the game. With you

dead, Gannon will never forgive me. He will never want to end the cat and mouse game between us."

Just yards from Nathan, a fireball exploded through a vent and spread to the ceiling. She heard him scream, but couldn't see beyond the wall of fire.

Heat made her dizzy and she could barely breathe now. She dropped to her knees by the back door and huddled next to Trevor. She didn't want to die.

"Darcy!"

In the distance, she imagined she heard Gannon and then the distant sound of sirens. She wondered if her mind was playing tricks on her.

She heard the crunch of metal and the sound of chain links snapping open.

The door suddenly opened. Sunlight and fresh air streamed into the room.

Darcy opened her eyes and saw Gannon's grim face staring down at her. He grabbed her by the shoulders and pulled her out of the fire. Leaving her on the cool grass, he ran back inside and dragged Trevor out.

Seconds later the church floor collapsed.

Chapter 15

Gannon moved Darcy a safe distance from the fire before he took her in his arms. He held her close to him. "Are you all right?"

She coughed, trying to suck in as much fresh air as her lungs would hold. "Yes. How's Trevor?"

Gannon glanced up. The EMTs had loaded Trevor onto a stretcher and had put an oxygen mask on his face. "He looks fine. They're taking good care of him."

"Good."

He stroked the sweat-dampened hair off her face as he glanced up at the church, now engulfed in flames. The tall spire topped with a cross groaned as its support structure started to give way.

Another couple of minutes and he'd have lost her today. "You shouldn't have come here alone."

She coughed and sat up. "I thought you needed me."

Anger ripped through him. "It wasn't me."

"It was Nathan," she said. "He is Nero."

"I know. I figured it out. That's why I came here."

Firefighters shot hoses of water onto the building. It couldn't be saved but they were worried about the fire spreading to the nearby woods. "I saw him at the front of the church. A fireball exploded and he was gone."

She shook her head. "This was all just a game to him."

He stroked her hair. "I know."

Stephen's angry voice rose above the noise of truck engines, sprays of water and men barking orders. "What do you mean—you're taking my tape?"

Gannon looked up and saw Chief Wheeler striding toward them. Stephen was right on his heels. "Get lost, Glass."

"Damn it, I want my tape." Glass looked at Gannon. "This nitwit thinks he can take my tape."

"It's evidence," the chief said.

"It's my tape and my story."

The chief lifted a brow. "My guess is that he wants the tape because it shows what we all saw— him running away from the fire while Darcy was still inside the church."

Gannon rose up and faced Stephen. "This is Darcy's story and if you try to steal it from her, I can guarantee that tape will end up on the six o'clock news."

Chief Wheeler grinned. "And seeing how popular you are, I bet it gets picked up all over the country."

Darcy stood. "You left us to die."

Stephen's eyes had lost their arrogance. "I was going for help."

Darcy shook her head. "You were running away from the building."

Gannon stepped between them before Stephen

could answer. "Leave now or I swear I'll take you apart piece by piece."

Stephen looked as if he'd argue, then backed down. "Fine. Nobody gives a damn about a year-old case." He stalked off.

Chief Wheeler tucked the tape in his jacket. "Looks like you are gonna get yourself some big attention from this story. Heck, I wouldn't be surprised if I don't see you getting interviewed on *Good Morning America*."

Darcy glanced up at Gannon. He couldn't read her expression, but he didn't have to. He realized the story that had brought her to him would take her away.

Chief Wheeler noticed the heavy silence between them. He cleared his throat. "Hey, I got work to do. You two be sure to stay away from the fire."

Gannon and Darcy nodded. When the chief had walked away, Gannon spoke first. Better to make this as easy as possible. "Look, I know this story is your big break. It's what you've always wanted."

She nodded. "A week ago, I'd have agreed with you."

He shoved out a breath. "And now?"

"It's still a story I want to write. And I will write it. But as for fame and fortune, I'm not convinced that suits me so much."

"What are you saying?"

She tucked a curl behind her ear. "I can write this story from anywhere. And well, Trevor and Mom need me. I was thinking I'd stay in Preston Springs for a while."

He grinned and laid his hands on her shoulders. "For a while?"

She hesitated. "Don't panic on me or anything. I don't want you to feel like I'm hemming you in."

"Darcy, we could stand here dancing around all afternoon, but I'm flat out of patience with games." He cupped her face in his hands. "I want you in my life."

She smiled. "I want to be in it."

Gannon kissed her on the lips. She wrapped her arms around his neck and relaxed into him as if she'd just arrived home from a long journey.

Epilogue

The Atlanta airport was packed. It was the Christmas season and everyone was looking to get somewhere.

In the small bookstore across from gate 32 on concourse A, Adrianna Ruiez juggled an armload of books that needed reshelving in the non-fiction section. Travelers often leafed through books and magazines to kill time before a flight and then abandoned them anywhere that suited.

Slobs, she thought ungraciously. If folks were just a little more considerate, she could sneak a few precious minutes studying for her chemistry final.

Adrianna was struggling with a couple of hardcover biographies when she heard a man clear his throat.

"Excuse me," the man said softly.

His politeness helped her manage a smile as she turned. "Yes, sir, what can I do to help you?" Her demeanor softened more when she looked at him. The man stood tall, wore neatly-pressed khakis, a white button-down shirt and thin wire-rimmed glasses that accentuated lovely green eyes. He carried a cane and wore a black leather glove on his right hand.

"I'm looking for a new book. It's non-fiction and called *Into the Fire*."

Adrianna smiled. "It's over here in the bestseller section. Follow me." Wishing she'd brushed her hair on her last break, she set her unshelved books down and guided him across the store. She noted he leaned heavily on the cane and walked with a decided limp.

She pulled the book from the shelf and handed him a copy. "Here you go."

He grinned as he studied the spine of the book and then opened the back flap and read the author's blurb. "Have you heard anything about the book?"

She wondered where he was traveling—somewhere important or exotic, no doubt. "I've not read it yet, but it's gotten great reviews."

He nodded. "With the cost of hardcovers these days, I don't buy books unless I think I'm really going to enjoy them. I've never heard of the author. Darcy Gannon?"

"Oh, she made a big splash on the news about a year ago. She solved an arson case. She ended up marrying one of the arson investigators just a couple of months ago."

He lifted a brow. "That so? How do you know so much about her?"

"There was a write-up on her in the Atlanta paper just a few days ago when the book came out."

"Too bad I missed it." He seemed to think for a moment. "That was the Nero case wasn't it?"

"Sure was."

A smile teased the edge of his lips. "Now I remember. This Darcy woman and her husband were the ones that didn't believe Nero was dead."

"Right. He faked his death in Washington, D.C., and would have gotten away with it all if he hadn't started his second round of fires."

He stared at her with an intensity that made her feel as if she were the only person in the world. "Some people never learn."

Adrianna sensed he knew more about the book than he was letting on. She wondered if asking for information on the book had been an excuse to meet her. "Can I ring it up for you?"

He studied the spine an extra beat. "Sure. And there's a book over there on puzzles. I think I'll get that, too."

"You like games?"

"Love 'em."

She caught a glimpse of the skin at his wrist. It was red and puckered as if it had been badly burned.

Adrianna watched the man limp toward the puzzle books. The guy looked fit. The limp must have been the result of an accident.

He approached the register, set his books on the counter and pulled his wallet out of his back pocket. He laid a hundred–dollar bill down.

She rang up his purchase. "So, where you headed?"

"West," he said. "I work construction and I've

got a few project managers who aren't doing what they're supposed to. I'm gonna show up unannounced and light a fire under them."

She sensed a private joke she wasn't privy to. She bagged up his purchase in a pink sack with Book Nook written on the side. "Hope you enjoy the book."

"I suspect I will enjoy every bit of this one." He took the change she offered and tucked it neatly into his pocket.

Not ready to see him go yet, Adrianna followed him toward the exit. She picked up a copy of *Into the Fire* from the bestseller table. She opened the book and flipped to the section in the middle where the pictures were. She'd not expected to see anything of interest but her gaze settled immediately on the head shot taken of Nero, aka Nathan Collier when he'd been in college.

Immediately, she was struck by the likeness between Nero and the stranger. "Hey, you look just like this guy Nero."

The stranger stopped and looked back at her. He grinned. "Imagine that."

The likeness really was eerie. But what were the

chances that Nero would be in the Atlanta airport where anyone could spot him? "Be careful, people might start calling you Nero."

The man seemed pleased by the idea. "Stranger things have happened."

Before she could say anything else, he limped into the crowd of people passing by her store and disappeared.

★ ★ ★ ★ ★

Deadly Secrets
Don't Stay Buried Forever

High-flying journalist Kelsey Warren has never forgiven her mother for abandoning her as a teen. Then Donna Warren's long-dead body—and evidence of her cold-blooded murder—resurfaces.

Despite Sheriff Mitch Garret's pleas to leave the case alone, Kelsey swears to find the truth. And as they come closer to uncovering the truth, someone is determined to silence Kelsey—*for good*.

M240_IDW

A simple town
A loving community
The perfect place for murder

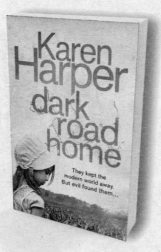

After a sinister case puts her life in danger, lawyer Brooke
seeks sanctuary in the quiet Amish town of Maplecreek.

But when four local teenagers are slaughtered, Brooke
can't abide by the community's stoic resolve to
mourn the dead in private.

Daniel left his childhood home to explore the outside
world. Now, returning to his Amish roots, he intends to
unmask his niece's killer and he'll need Brooke's help…
They could be Maplecreek's last hope as a deadly threat
to their peaceful world closes in.

www.mirabooks.co.uk

THE SINS OF THE PAST
SHALL NOT BE FORGIVEN...

The shocking murder of local 'saint' Sister Anne
draws the attention of reporter Jason Wade. He is
sure the police are hunting the wrong man – and
it's up to him to track down the real killer.

And then his father's demons reveal a story so
twisted Jason will need all his wits to
untangle the truth.

The thrilling third novel featuring reporter Jason Wade

www.mirabooks.co.uk

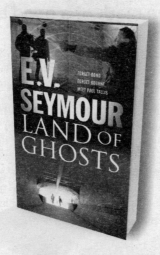

MIRA

The mark of a good book

At MIRA we're proud of the books we publish, that's why whenever you see the MIRA star on one of our books, you can be assured of its quality and our dedication to bringing you the best books. From romance to crime to those that ask, "What would you do?" Whatever you're in the mood for and however you want to read it, we've got the book for you!

Visit **www.mirabooks.co.uk** and let us help you choose your next book.

★ **Read** extracts from our recently published titles

★ **Enter** competitions and prize draws to win signed books and more

★ **Watch** video clips of interviews and readings with our authors

★ **Download** our reading guides for your book group

★ **Sign up** to our newsletter to get helpful recommendations and **exclusive discounts** on books you might like to read next

www.mirabooks.co.uk